AF254448

Remembering
The
World

Remembering The World

Place Given Poems

by

Bob Mustin

Copyright © 2019 Bob Mustin

ISBN: 978-1-64516-134-9

Library of Congress Number: 2019903245

All rights reserved. No part of this book may be produced or transmitted in any form, or by any means, electronic or mechanical, including photocopying, or by any information storage system without permission in writing from the publisher or author.

First published by Gridley Fires Books,
4/15/2019

Cover design by Lacey O'Connor
Interior art by Lucy Teague
Edited by Bob Mustin

What do we do
Given life?
We move around

~ *Move Around* ~
Stephen Stills

Contents

By Way of Explanation

We live in a fragmented world. This isn't to say the planet is in a state of devolution, but my view of it may mean we've reached the limits of world culture as it's developed to this point. If you need to blame something for this state of affairs, however, blame the Enlightenment. After all, it was those thinkers who fostered the idea that we can best understand reality by breaking it down into its constituent parts. What was lost in their pursuits is the fact that the whole, if I may embellish a cliché, is greater and far more wondrous than a summation of its parts.

The world, whom we more readily know by the ancient name, Gaia, the sublimely intelligent being that serves as our host in the conglomeration of Universe, has ways of resolving the complications of difficult free riders such as us. A dog has disease-prone fleas, and it scratches until at least some retire to their primal home in the grasses. A hippo serves as a sub-Saharan taxi for the oxpecker bird, which in turn eats parasites from the hippo's leathery skin. In much the same way, Gaia's plant, animal, and mineral kingdoms serve as both bane and blessing for humanity. Tempestuous she is, but she gives us great beauty, and at times an idyllic life.

Her geology, however, is rife with evidence that we have occasionally treated her unkindly. Like a caring parent, she imposes restrictions on us. First the gentler ones, increasing their severity until we wake up to understanding her, respecting and loving her. Or, too late, we retire to a primitive state to live out Plan B. If we've devised one.

Our impact, however, wouldn't be as great, for both good and bad, if we didn't travel. Our innate mobility lets us move with the vagaries of the seasons, the years, the eras. We travel, we settle down, we evolve. This makes us strong yet different. It makes us, well, interesting to one another. And it seems to allow us to fear one another.

I was reared in a military family, and with that began a life of travel. I've taken hundreds of pictures of what to me are exotic locales, bought picture postcards and the equally old-fashioned slides to help jog my memory of those places. As youth abandoned me and adulthood began to ask more thoughtfulness of me, I turned to writing scanty travel notes to supplement memory. These weren't intended to be scintillating prose; they were means to memory's end. Many have been random reactions to the beautiful, the famous, the usual and unusual. Scenic depictions. Humorous encounters. The deep, inner feelings Gaia's powerful places generate within me.

Besides providing the usual tourist's sops for memory, some have found their way into poetic form. I present a fraction of them here in an attempt at piecing together memory's fragments into a workable view of life on Gaia. Some are a bit polemical, others tinged with irony. Some have a wry undergirding, and still others paint unvarnished pictures of what we think about and talk about and act on in the presence of our planetary host. I've seen love in its many forms in my travels, I've seen the impacts, the travesties of war, and much in between.

The relevant question, then, is why do I bother to put them into poems and, more to the point, why this publication? It's my work, I think, as an observer and writer to see the world as it is and to wonder what's missing, what keeps it in such a fragmented state. I have the feeling that ours was once one cohesive world. If this is so, I want to do what I can to re-member it. Further, poetry allows much meaning with fewer words. So perhaps by correctly selecting bits and pieces I've experienced of life, clues to its re-membering will emerge from some faint state of wholeness that remains. In the end, this is all I alone can hope to do.

Places given with each poem are the source of the poem's soul. Dates given are either the date of encounter with that source, or that of the inspiration or the initial writing.

Bob Mustin

Moving Around

Gold Rush

Sacramento, CA
August 1995

Why are we gathered
at the edge of the world
where waves crash
where bedrock shivers
eyes to the horizon
for the next new thing?

Floods, fires, and quakes
nothing could deter
us from this our Eden.
We heard destiny's voice
magnetic from horseback
in Conestogas rolling
toward paradise.

Here, precious stones
glittered like Ba'al.
We built speakeasies
mansions, banks
nothing now
but a handful
of waning promise.

Today shop doors creak
trucks groan, unload.
We sip our coffee
and still we wait
the rush of dawn
golden on our backs.

The Day Kennedy Died

U.S. Naval Academy,
Annapolis, MD
November 1983

Leaves are falling
and I must write a letter.

Yawls and knockabouts
sails a-luff. Mind full
a gale of thoughts

hang of hair shine of shoes
classes going by
like twelve-inch shells.

The letter's not going well.
A thousand reasons
arguing whispering

Quit this place this history.

But the damning questions
What is Duty?
Honor? Fidelity?

"They got him,"
an upperclassman said.

I know his thoughts
frightening
as Hell itself.

A gull glides to a dot
settles on a yardarm
its call faint insistent.

Before the ink is dry
I leave that place.

Mexico Lindo

Chetumal, Mexico
August 1996

"Fernando, play your guitar, sing for us,"
the loud Americans say. We throw money.
"It's our custom to pay the piper
to hell with sensibility – we're having fun."

They spill their margaritas
the sticky alcoholic sheen
reflects a cradle of palm fronds
holding a forlorn moon.

Fernando smiles. He is patient and good.
"*La canción es muy bonita,*" someone says
"*me gusta, me encanta.*" Winds have sung
across the Yucatan have followed rain

into the jungle the tangles of memory.
Those remaining embrace a plaintive dance
Mi corazon no me habla – birds speak of it
take refuge from the night.

Downeast - Acadia

Acadia National Park, ME
October 1998

You think *I* seem reckless?
Don't you feel the howl
like a semi doing ninety
adrenaline on rampage
its spittle on your glasses?

It's the perfect time to shoot
those birches. Roots gnaw
at stone lithe branches
dance, a tousled cowlick.

Will you listen? This wind
fails to move that island
from my horizon each
rock unwilling to submit
to a fractious Atlantic.

It's dangerous here
at Thunder Hole too.
I shiver savor its hunger
as it gulps a rush of tide.

One tenacious gull provides
a final photo op. She yaws
suspended in a last
determined pose. A gust
takes her from my lens.

Sycamore

Decatur, GA
July 1999

His days at the end
fragile lifeblood thin
days of constant naps
and an old man's stories.

I watched him wither
cracked skin loose.
Beneath, variegations
and rainbowed bruises
the map of eighty seasons.

My last visit I tied up
his loose ends – raked his yard
wrote his youngest son.
Then we talked of other things.

Space heater a humming
ember he thought it was
summer pointed said he'd
made the bench beneath
the sycamore from heart pine.

Its shade was always cool
broad leaves a host
of leathery hands set
to applaud each breeze.

Living in Monet

Decatur, GA
August 1998

Walking though autumn
liberated from sweat's glue
iced tea baseball
and watermelon the mercy
of Southern summers.

Another season recalled
pieces of Giverny's garden
bridge above water lilies
the music of lapping
waves in oily pigments

each brushstroke so precise
so full a world born
within each one.
Squint and together
they make sense.

Is this mere recall
a cheap memento
of what was
or a promise
of what will be?

Beneath fingerlocked
branches an arch across
a broad suburban street
broken acorn-stained
walks. How am I
to live in this world?

This masterpiece
this hologram
a mere illusion
an *oeuvre* in progress.

We are neither
meant to be nor
accident neither
here nor there
neither bound
nor free.

The truth?
We were born
tabula rasa
groping blind.

Unseen hands work
through us
each another
brushstroke
on pure white canvas.

Images

Imagination
(In Memory of Richard Brautigan)

Atlanta, GA
June 1984

Watch a cloud float by
trim its Grecian gods away
unmask its inner nothing
filled with sheer bouquets.

When the time is right
summon back the gods
watch them plait shadows
into your sun-wet hair.

I should have called this poem LOVE.

Portrait of a Dancer

Biloxi, MS
November 1996

photograph
in white – canted
frame complements
TV's gray state

at sixteen
enigmatic smile
skinny-legged diamond
a perfect plié

legs grown
listless now she
lives in memory
TV's eye blank

her two closed
head bowed
dreaming ardor back
into the dance

Fraulein Angelika

Inspired by
Ron Hansen's novel,
Hitler's Niece,
Asheville, NC
September 1999

I'm your uncle he said
almost a stranger.

He lingered months
bought her licorice and dresses
she played her piano sang

infected his thoughts
with urges far outside
the gates of innocence.

One night he crept
into her bed begged
for a special kiss

and she begged too
before they found her
the gun the lying note

proclaiming pain is never
divorced from pleasure.

The Way the Sun Sets

After Munch's
"The Scream"
Asheville, NC
March 2005

I dread the sun going down.
I'm afraid I'll fall with it
over the edge of the world
the sun's afraid, too – see
the way it swells surrenders

to a sea of its own making?
I have to hold tight or it's
over the rail into the bay
into that swirl of ships
shrinking to nothing.

Don't you hear it too?
Don't you feel it
the groans the gravity
of fingers dragging us
to horizon's line?

It's hard to watch to feel
the moment. But that's
the way the sun sets
yellow with plasma
red with blood.

Plath

Asheville, NC
April 2006

A field of hunger
beyond her window
wet in the thin
light of morning.

Oxeyes and black-eyed Susans
lean sunward
grasping captive
to finespun stems.

Pendulous as roses, she muses
caught between a blue
forever and tangles
of bloody briars.

They share her loss
her quest
for something
precious beyond
all reach.

Heaven Waits

Inspired by a 15th century
Chinese painting
Atlanta, GA
April 1998

Dai Jin has seen
the mountain
from the river.
Footpath upward
to a grotto. Switchback
step-stones crowned

in dust wind through
solitary cedars green
drops of sweat hanging
from untamed scarps.
Roots search hardscrabble
for eternity.

The grotto numinous
doorway to heaven
waits.

No he says this is
far enough.
I have walked the Dao
now I must paint.

A Letter to Papa

Inspired by
A Moveable Feast,
Asheville, NC
July 2004

Dear Ernest,

Words fail me. Your one
good sentence sometimes
seems an unreachable goal.
Still we the generations
that follow write as if
this pursuit alone could bind
our truths to yours.

Beneath that one good sentence
the urge to live to understand
with liberating clarity
We bear failure when we must
wear fame with caution
these the only rightful stripes
the only true rewards.

One last thought to submit.
We who weigh ourselves
with words enter many
worlds, some battlefields
some clean well-lighted places
but few have lived the craft
as well as you.

Pasternak

One cannot forget the fear
That furrowed all those faces.
From *Fearful Tale*
Asheville, NC
September 2002

A field of simple order
pierced by a single fir
staunch against fire and storm.
In its shadow Russian hands

break clods of blood earth.
The fir tree their cross
their emblematic longing
twice-sown cabbage

wheat and potatoes remain
their humble ambition. Noon comes.
Mopped sweat on ragged sleeves
and once more the clank of war.

Faces turn skyward. A sea
of empty hearts discharges
prayers in timeless song
"Please Lord deliver us."

Arms out knees rooted
their chant becomes
an inner hum as souls
prepare to take wing.

The fir tree whispers
"Stop your mewling!
Do you need such comfort?
Today you discover heaven."

The Way Our World Will End

Between the idea
And the reality
Between the motion
And the act
Falls the Shadow
T.S. Eliot in
"The Hollow Men"
Decatur, GA
March 2000

She was shy well-heeled
a pretty piece of verse
in need of a reading.

We talked across our canapes
and warm champagne

and the matchmakers smiled
from across the room
gods admiring their creation.

Two years later still
gorgeous from the swelling

her smile a buoyant sun
she held him out
for me to hold.

He wasn't trouble then
the way he was at fourteen.

She speaks of him tenderly
in pontifical "we"s as if
his fate could have been altered

with rote articulation
with prayers to broken stones.

I find myself in lust
for the way we were
an emasculated soul.

It's three A.M. sleep
once more a fugitive

but there can be no rest.
Unspoken words hover
she in her world, I in mine.

Random Moods

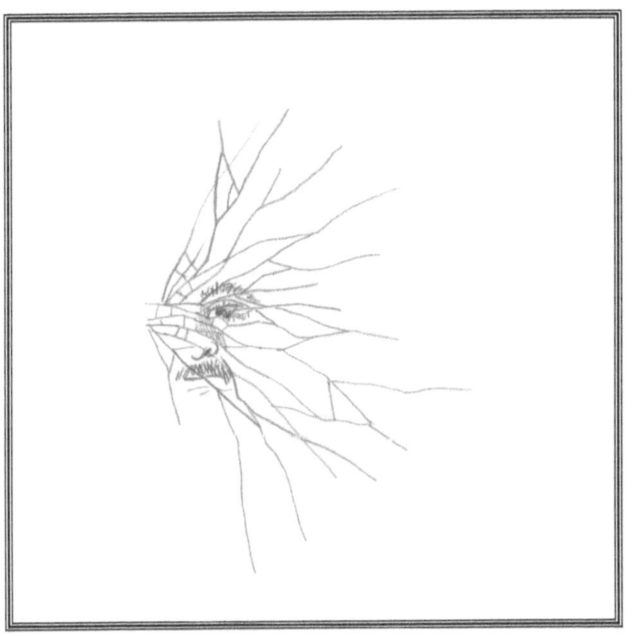

Mirror With Cracks

Weaverville, NC
February 2003

These strikes a slowly
formed topography.
Time's erosion painted
in alchemy's blood. Hints
of red and blue and yellow
spawn a jigsawed image
a face an odd amalgam mine.

The eyes probing faded
try to plumb memory
to a time before cracks formed
before the singleness of youth
gave to so many disparate lives
left me to wonder why
this is the one revealed.

Truth

Albuquerque, NM
October 2000

What is truth? Where is it found?
Through virtue? No.
That one wears a wanton look.
Heaven's narrow compass? All bets
are off on judgment day.

A newsstand near work – last chance
for tabloid revelation.
Three bucks for greasy coffee
strudel to fuel this gas.

Something in me wants to taste
the sex life of movie stars
grace an e.t.'s operating table
and how would it feel
to be Hitler's love child?

"A truth that's told with bad intent
bests all the lies you can invent."
said William Blake making
the case for deconstruction.

We step lightly as we probe
the void between two points
of certainty the living ground
between opposing poles.

The search must start somewhere.

Grumblings

Atlanta, GA
January 2000

January speaks of war.
Sun assails the earth's slant
opens veins of rime. Sundown
frost regroups readies its attack.

Dawn today. Peasant doves
peck at frostbitten seeds
my houseshoes couldn't help
but trample on the way
to pick up the paper.

Now its drivetime news
morning drivers locked in
metal combat. A wren outside
my breakfast nook begs alms.

On the deck railing
the squirrel feeder lid
claps like cannon fire.
Bushytails upturn peanut
hulls in their scavenge.

Below, I'm sure to find
finches have ejected spent
thistle shells onto rows
of late beets and turnips

torched by last night's frost.
Who can unearth serenity in this?
Maybe an answer lies hidden
in the classifieds page two
an opportunity I can't pass up.

Metamorphosis I

Atlanta, GA
October 1999

Vapor rises to grace the sun
condensed its jewels gleam
sleep exposes coarser thoughts
refines them into dreams.

Progress is a fragile child
a quirk a rare design
most things we achieve
are accidents in time.

Marketplace Evangelism

Atlanta, GA
October 1999

We were his captives – a motivational speaker
prowling the stage, microphone in hand.

We found much to mull in his patter.
Tales of merchandising schemes gone bad

how to flush our quarry from legal cover.
We laughed at the innocent their foibles

nodded self-assuredly
charted our own pathways

through the hunting fields of commerce.
Then soothing music flooded us.

He stirred us with a tender benediction
beseeching us to stalk our destiny.

We left, hunters within his firmament
lumps in our throats the size of sated hunger.

Fire

Atlanta, GA
December 1970

Strange the way fire attracts
as if it were a new idea.

A moth approaches center stage
trims its sails and dives.

I wonder – does its immolation
presage mine?

I see myself stumble
along dark paths until

my tolerance for gloom
consumes me.

Te Deum For the Muses

Asheville, NC
April 1996

Morning, madams
I'm a hack musician
something better
as a trafficker in words.

You come well
recommended
I heard some of what
you've inspired

in the music
of a guy named Homer
and it really plucked
my inner strings.

So I was thinking.
Could we do lunch
sometime? Have a shot
of ouzo and jam?

Warming Wood

Fayetteville, GA
December 1994

They say wood
warms you twice
once when the chainsaw
barks, spitting dust
its teeth traversing years
measured against the grain
your every fiber supple
your cheeks two rising suns.

And again when you press
a match to the tinder
the heat returns
embraces you with
limber arms its glow
revealing the work
of decades etched
across your face.

Drunk

Atlanta, GA
November 1968

The horse's name
on this carousel? Helpless.
A man beyond pleasure
blinks his bathroom mirror's
truth into focus.

An off-key calliope
un cavalier, tombe.
The rider falls
white fixtures
pass slowly as time
on the way down.

Does the horse notice?
Not in her wooden state.
Were her soul more
tender she would
rescue him.

The Rubber Knife

Atlanta, GA,
October 1968

A prank, I told the teacher. See?
The blade bends a joke of rubber.

She took it and at supper
man I heard about it.

The sergeant hovered
a baleful presence.
"You threatened little girls?"

"Just a little," I said.
"You scare Mama all the time."

Later she asked me
if the whipping hurt.

"No ma'am," the belt
still hard against me.
"I just tuned it out."

She frowned. "I'm glad
your teacher has the knife.
You're too much like your father."

Broccoli

Dallas, TX
May 1996

You know its quandary
as well as I – thick neck
stretches upward
gropes for the sun

hydra-head unfolds
a thousand eyes search
find only questions.

Roots web and burrow
thirsty as summer's burn.
A pair of fates compete
for possession of its soul

to be hacked and eaten
or to last till autumn
florets falling eyes blind.

Metamorphosis II

Atlanta, GA
October 1999

When a city is born
no bands play.
No wing-to-wing fly-bys
only the alligator crawl
of scaly machines.

Something ominous
owns the mouse-gray
sky today something
opposed to the habits
of a waxing sun.

Machu Picchu rose
to greet the sun-god.
His praise rained down
strong as peasant labor
until only bones remain.

Light and Leaves

Decatur, GA
October 1968

Sun's incursion
into my trees
a battleground where
photosynthesis
writes the treaty
between light and leaves.

I'm a spy exposed
daylight's captive
my shadowy excesses
gone naked. New moon
the nimble fingers
of night will spring me.

The King of Hell

Asheville, NC
April 2002

He has this pickled
breath a cucumber nose
a fly has settled on
and it seems he's set
to kill the bastard.

He eyes me coughs
expelling a gamy vapor.
Does he mean to speak?
No taken with the fly I think.
I smile and say hello.

"Who the hell are you?"
he thunders. "No one really.
I'm recently divorced you see
and the last thing my ex said was
I should visit this place."

"You see this goddamn fly?"
I decide to indulge so I nod.
"Come closer," he insists.
Another flagpole-wilting breath.
I shake my head. No!

From my perspective
encounters shouldn't be
this torturous. Maybe
I was better off in the more
familiar hell at home.

Waiting For Home

On This Lake
(Canadian Border Crossing)

Lake Saganaga, MN
June 1969

On this lake
rumpled flannel

twists of sinew
flexing. My paddle
digs relaxes floats.

A stand of poplar
hurries by.

Now a breeze
to wake the waters
a muted loon croaks.

I wish to linger
no future here
no past

a single moment
newborn undivided.

Something Inside

Portland, ME
November 1997

A ragged quilt of clouds
across the harbor

a frail sun lurks
behind this morning pall.

Something else: the smell
of fish is everywhere.

The plaint of gulls
echoes wharf to wharf

srarved for some vile
wretched thing.

Tattooed boys and girls
conspire in whispers

glance up sip
their three-buck coffees.

Still the loathsome smell.
The breeze can't dispel it.

Can a town be this cheerless?
God, I have to go.

Navigating streets
broken asphalt streams

my rental car leaves
a wake of paper.

At last the highway.
A scrap of humanity

clings to a signpost.
He tents his dirty tatters

fumbles out a half-
gone cigarette.

Hurry safe now
rearview mirror check

putrescence a dot behind.
Too late for me though.

Something inside
distance can't cleanse.

It's Christmas and We Don't Know Each Other

Decatur, GA
Christmas 1999

A late sleep, a day off suspended breath
for an anxious world. Next door they've risen

prodded by coffee the ritual before them
as predictable as marital sex.

We don't know each other. I have no specifics
but there's laughter and a door slams shut.

At the curb a tree too soon abandoned.
Metal icicles wave wink at the sun

balloons of paper broken boxes
a bag of last year's toys.

Soon it'll be over then back to work
or at least the usual isolation.

The wind howls its upset. I shiver
throw on a log from a dwindling stack.

I should walk but not in this weather.
Across the street the cat wants in.

Think I'll make a call or two and read.
Holidays run long in the suburbs.

The Real Thing

Atlanta, GA
April 2000

Cobwebs hang where thoughts raced
doctor's orders, damn him.
Nothing like the adrenaline rush
of caffeine. Ventricles pump
to force fifty years
of living into every hour.

No coffee here. Suisse Mocha
chai latte such poor substitutes.
Sneak a strong cup of tea
for breakfast and don't forget
the large Coke with lunch.

Truth will tell: mind a fine machine
should run full tilt from the start.
No stagnant pool of dull pretensions.
The world turns new each day
and here I am daydreaming

daydreaming about a steak
not tofu and vegetables and who
drinks beet juice anyway?
There's purity in milk and sugar
the smell of freshly-ground robusta.

Somewhere the real thing survives.

Sanctuary

Lake Fork, TX
Thanksgiving 1998

The war began covertly.
Steel thorns among reeds
sun climbing a hogback ridge
over pines and poplars.

Thunder booming staccato.
We shrank from the echoes
refused the hunter's celebration –
feather-bursts bodies in falling arcs.

From hearthside we listened mute
took refuge in sandwiches and coffee
buried our thoughts in books
until the sun turned to scarlet coal.

Then a stealth of mallards at water's
edge thirteen of them drifting.
Buoyed we stoked the fire
pulled up our afghans and drowsed.

A Postal Story

An incident
Decatur, GA
August 2017

He was the nicest man you'd ever meet
a witness said. He took his kids
to church and helped them do homework.
Everyone who knew him liked him.

I know we didn't see it coming.
Lord there's wickedness enough
we shun darkness when we can
always let the sunshine in.

Sure he had his quirks.
I only wish you'd known him
maybe you'd understand. He wasn't
so different from you and me.

Japanese Garden

Portland, OR
October 1997

Nothing here exists
by happenstance.
Azalea blooms –
silence tumbling
in rivulets
to a sunning pond.

Pines and bonsai maples
mute the rattle
of bamboo deer guards.
Bashful rakers
bend to waves
of white stone.

A boy laughs.
Water gossips
over rocks.
He bids it hush
into the grassy carpet
we tiptoe across.

A bridge meant
to baffle demons
zigzags
across a pond
and eddies
of hungry carp.

The teahouse today –
empty. It holds a silent
rite invisible
released into
nonexistent cups.

Beyond the gate
we notice clouds
try not to hurry
confident
the looming rain
will hold.

Missing You

Quintana Roo, Mexico
August 1995

There were visas and baggage checks
sometimes the border guards smiled
and long lines of brown faces
wound toward the setting sun.
I spent the day making
cheap conversation and as
darkness swallowed me I knew
I was missing you.

The night grew hollow and quiet
but soon a casita and dinner
and I slept carried away like
reggae on a Jamaican breeze.
Waking inside this dream
I reached out thirsting
and the taste told me
I was missing you.

Acknowledgements

The following appeared in the indicated publications in altered forms:

"Warming Wood," *The Reach of Song, 1996-1997*, Georgia State Poetry Society, Inc., p. 24
"Fraulein Angelika," "Upon This Lake," "Marketing Ploy," *Niederngasse,* www.niederngasse.com. "Marketing Ploy" was also published in a print edition of *Niederngasse,* Issue 5, January 2000, p.11
"King of Hell," *Grab-a-Nickel*, Volume XXXXIII, Number 6, Spring/Summer 2003, pub. Barbour County Writer's Workshop and Alderson Broadus College, p.17
"Fire," *The Green Tricycle*, http://greentricycle. com/8ring7.html
"Broccoli," Poetry Midwest, Number 6, Winter 2003, www.poetrymidwest.org, p.39

"Warming Wood" won 3rd Place in the Ninth Annual Byron Herbert Reece International Awards, sponsored by The Georgia State Poetry Society, 1996-1997

Bob Mustin has had a brief naval career and a longer one as a civil engineer and has been a North Carolina Writers Network writer-in-residence at Peace College under the late Doris Betts' guiding hand. In the early 90s he was the editor of a small literary journal, *The Rural Sophisticate*, based in Georgia. His work has appeared extensively in print and electronic publications.

To learn more about Bob Mustin, visit
Website: www.gridleyfiresbooks.com
Blog: bobmust.wordpress.com

ISBN-13: 978-1-7643223-0-0

First edition: February 28 2026. Cover art: Heidi Monsant
Editing assistance: Laura Wilkinson

2

The Pirate and the Panopticon

A novella by

Katherine Clark

To my mum. Thank you for always reading my work, even as a
teen writing terrible x-men fanfiction.

This novella is dedicated to all those who need to escape.

Whether it be a bad day, a break-up, an exhausting work meeting,
or the Panopticon.

1. The Outside

We were destined to end in tragedy.

All magic-dealers were, but the gods cursed those who dealt by sea the most.

It was why I had no qualms facing death. I expected it.

I already missed the ocean, but it couldn't survive the desert. The sea perished endless miles ago. Water turned extinct – only dry sand and harsh heat prevailed. Those gods didn't dare moisten the sand beneath me, for it wasn't theirs to control.

The Desert God owned this land. He governed the barren desert, the wastelands and vast nothingness. The god had a name, but I didn't dare even think it as I perched atop a dune, staring at his eternal, oppressive space, searching across the torrid orange. Only fools spoke their names – fools and pets. Only one of those applied to me.

His land was utterly dry, the air whispering only a hint of humidity. There would've been no moisture, nothing to quench the thirst of the forsaken eyeless animals that roamed these dunes past sunset, if it weren't for the thick droplets of sweat that rolled down my forehead, my neck, captured on my cream linen tunic.

I wiped my forehead, the sun boiling with wrathful god eyes. I had already moved for too long, just to wear time's curse. Smatterings of boils covered my tanned skin, and welts prickled exposed flesh, the dry air an unrelenting warning. Hesitating, I wrapped my headscarf tighter around my face as though it weren't too late.

I couldn't afford to lose so much liquid, not when I still hadn't found the entrance.

The Panopticon's entrance was concealed from the mere mortal eye. Only a seer or someone with the golden monocular could find it. I was no seer, but magic-dealing had its advantages, even if it was why we were in this mess.

I unclipped the golden monocular from my belt, considering the rare trinket. Not rounded like other monoculars, no, it held sharpened edges. So sharp, one had to hover the device a few inches away from their eye to use it. The monocular cooled as though it existed in an ocean, not the desert. Gold gilded on top of leather and glass, the lens a delicate crystal. A test, and many mortals lost an eye by being too greedy. Magic always held a lesson.

Breathing out, I steadied my heart and placed the sharpened edge to my left eye, hovering the razor edge away. Magic seeped through my sight. Prickles of electricity throbbed, poking my mind, as I breathed in a slightly bitter scent. It hummed, but I didn't dare let it touch me. I couldn't afford to lose my other eye, as my right had been stolen long ago.

The hilltop overlooked a vastness of rolling orange dunes, endless and oppressively similar, like movement made no progress.

I tried not to think of my life, of him, not yet, as I scanned the thick golden dust covering the rolling dunes, the sky so dull it blended as though the ground had no end, but his face lingered.

"Farrah." The man looked at me with utter fear.

He was burly, thickly built, with long brown hair far too silky for the brutish body it lay over. The locks landed delicately over scarred skin. Many refused to meet his gaze, but not I. I didn't falter, not as I stared right back at those golden-brown eyes and narrowed my blue one in return.

"Ant, no." I used the nickname he so heavily hated others using, but not I.

Most men didn't like to look at me. I didn't wear an eyepatch like other pirates. The dark fabric sat too warmly, too oppressively on top of useless flesh. My eye deserved its mourning, and the other pirates could shove their stares up their cannons.

The empty eye was a chasm of pale pink flesh, but Antorn never looked away. He looked at me as though nothing was missing, that I was utterly complete. He didn't just stare into my one eye, no, he met both. The sea blue and emptiness.

Something shifted. Something told me that as time waned, we lost it. Smoke built.

"Farrah, you must go!" he said, though he knew I wouldn't.

That was why he stuck a dagger in my side and kicked me off the ship with his leather boot.

I barrelled downwards and slammed into the ocean. My blood coated the thin membrane top of the turquoise water without permission, the salty liquid like knives on my newly carved flesh. I floated. The ocean's salt content so high that a month-old corpse would float. The blade rested in my flesh, plugging pain from my body and my heart.

Bastard.

That blade sat on the left side of my belt, purring to be used. A dagger – a well-crafted dagger. Ant's dagger.

I shook off the memories. I had no time for sentimentality. My hand grazed the left side of my tunic, feeling the tender spot where several fading stitches now hugged closed skin. The bastard saved my life, and I hated him so much for it. Now, I'd return the favour.

A mortal eye would see nothing, but the golden monocular revealed the truth. The orange sky deepened, dunes casting slight shadows on top of the nearby burrows. But there, that one. One burrow didn't resemble the others made by ravenous, thirsty creatures. Instead, the burrow presented as a flawless semicircle peeking from a small hill. Not only perfectly round, but it glittered with the monocular's power, tiny speckles of white light fluttering with the stagnant breeze. It looked wet. Moisture lasted several steps before the burrow, covering its perfectly circular walls.

The water was a trick, aimed at luring those foolish enough to survive this desert, foolish enough to take respite on their way to the prison.

The water intended to trick me.

I may have only one eye, but no magic trick would work on me. Never again.

Without the monocular, it looked utterly ordinary, but with it, the lens detected magic. Good. Progress teased like a myth, too slippery to grasp, until now.

Sand sifted beneath my brown boots, my pants tucked firmly into the leather, as I trudged forward. I couldn't control losing sweat, but I needed to contain my blood. No way would the dust ticks suckle against my ankles and drain me before I even started this reckless mission.

The monocular hovered near my eye, confirming with a fervent frequency that the approaching burrow still glittered. Sand thickened the further I moved. Not quite quicksand but dense enough that it took a measurable force to lift each foot and advance. Grunting, I fought my slowing pace.

The eyeless animals, the sandivores, considered me from their makeshift burrows with fierce red mouths. They wouldn't attack, not yet, not when the sun still painted the sky. I tapped my dagger, the dagger that only weeks earlier had worn my blood, a reminder of my protection. But I couldn't afford to waste energy on those primal beasts.

All I had was my body, my weapon and a few magic trinkets resting against a thick brown belt that fastened my pants to my cream tunic. I had spent every last coin – mostly counterfeit – preparing my body for this moment.

Weeks prior, my body was thin, frail. Now, I was thicker, tougher, stronger. I needed strength to carry forward, to get through the seven levels of the Panopticon. I needed brute force.

Truthfully, I needed Ant. But that wasn't possible.

He was the reason I was here.

I lifted my feet higher, wading through the sand before it devoured me, bounding through its viscosity.

Ant: Prisoner of the Panopticon. I thought of him again, the memory that got us here unshakeable.

1 DAY UNTIL CAPTURE:

"This is magnificent, Farrah." Ant gripped my shoulders so tightly that my bones ached.

We both had gotten too lean in this last adventure, though Ant's thick build was almost otherworldly, and he still towered in size over the men of the Rain Isles. For Ant, it had been worth it. We'd done it. We'd procured the rarest magic item known to mortals. Some gods didn't know this existed. Cirrus, the Rain God, kept this creation to herself for thousands of years. Until we found it.

Only Ant didn't whimper when he whispered the name of a god. In fact, he sought to face one.

The only mortals who breathed their names were already dead, even if they didn't know it yet.

Ant grinned, my skin shivering in anticipation. Not because of the ocean and rainwater coating our bodies, not because of the darkness, icy wind, the isolation. This was wrong. We would surely piss off the wrong god, and worse, piss off the Ovators. I had let Ant's obsession blind me. And now that we had what we sought, the truth rattled me.

"Why do you look so troubled?" Ant's eyes darted between my blue eye and my empty socket. Despite the missing eye, the eyebrow often gave away my truth.

"This is a bad idea."

And it absolutely had been. Of course, I was right. I was always right.

As I reached the burrow's opening, glittering sand hissed, urging me to retreat. I wouldn't.

The orange sun fell half below the horizon. It wouldn't be long until the creatures of the night joined me. I needed to move fast, for as soon as the sun retreated, darkness would own this land.

I tapped my belt with a sigh. No magic trinket could fight against that glittering wet sand, at least nothing on me. And it surrounded the entrance. Everything I brought was carefully deliberated – no food, no water. None left, at least. The only liquid coated my brown lens.

I should wear it, should place that lens in my eye. Blue was valuable. Even the Panopticon prisoners would fight for it. My eye shone the colour of the sea. Blue no longer existed in this desert, not even the sky dared to share the shade. I picked out the lens and threw its liquid over the burrow's sand and watched.

Nothing at first. The liquid was so minimal. But then… the hiss.

The hiss grew – it boiled. At first, the sand flickered golden, then deep crimson, before it faded to grey. The small circle where the liquid met the wet sand proved the hypothesis. Deep magic protected this entrance.

I needed to destroy the wetness.

10

My feet pressed firmly into the sand, ankles almost grazing the top. Dust ticks whistled at my feet. Small, slimy red things that looked like magnified blood. I grunted. I didn't like this, didn't want to lose even a shred of precious liquid blood. But I had no choice, no way to jump the wet sand, no way to slide within the burrow without potentially losing a limb.

My hand trembled as I lifted my left pant leg.

What an absurd fear. What had Ant said to me?

"Fear is what sets us apart from the gods, Farrah."

I embraced my mortality as the minuscule slimy bastards began feasting on my flesh. The sensation built like tiny bursts of pressure, ending in a prickle of pain. They sucked pale skin. Years at sea with the sun pouring down on my shoulders had created an array of shades across my body. The places the sun couldn't touch were the many wounds that lined my body in delicate, thunderous patterns. Each blemish told a story. The one lining my left calf appeared a favoured, delicious spot, with swarms of dust ticks sucking between the white raised scar tissue.

Enough, that was enough. I unclipped a black leather glove from my belt and slid it on. It hugged tightly, restricting. One by one, I peeled the dust tick, flinging them onto the shimmering sand.

They did not fizz, not at first. They drank. Dumb little brainless things, but instinct warned of the fatal magic. They wouldn't seek it, but once forced on top of it, they were ravenous. They drained the magic liquid before erupting in fleeting orange flames. One by one, I flicked the dust ticks, careful that they landed in different spots. Those spots dried. It took dozens, and I lost too much blood, but eventually, as I grabbed the last dust tick that suckled on my scar tissue, pushing down my pant leg, and flung it further than all the others, an obvious dried grey path materialised.

Menacing orange lined the narrow grey path. They were tiny insects after all, the path wide enough for a single foot, and the tunnel's top still glimmered with wet magic, but it would do. I could go another round, but my leg already cautioned with prickles of red.

Sweating and bloody, not the combination I wanted, not yet. Although – inevitable. One didn't break in and traverse a prison unscathed.

I hurled the lens onto the ground, defiant in the action. Let them try to take my eye. Their desperation made them weak. This was not a mission I expected to survive. No water, no food, no lens, just a fool in love.

Destined to end in tragedy.

The first time Ant told me he loved me came to the front of my mind as I walked the dried sand as though I walked the plank.

Funnily enough – a very similar scenario.

1903 DAYS UNTIL CAPTURE:

"Fuck you, Ant," I seethed.

Our ship floated above deep ocean. The blue hues cascaded into navy before darkness destroyed colour. Only the slap of the waves carried the nearby shore's azure tint. We weren't far out, but beneath us lay the merfolk, and the water needed to be deep to hold their entire kingdom.

Salt burned my blue eye as I narrowed it towards my usurper.

Ant stood at the base of the plank with feet firmly settled on the ship's stable wooden ground. My ship. Was he really planning to lead a mutiny? To take this ship over? Even after sharing my hammock? My body waved as the plank swayed in the cool breeze. I raised my arms to steady myself.

My entire crew – the unified group of idiot assholes – watched, snickering. Actually snickering. The rage shone on my face in flecks of red, gathering closely at the bridge of my nose. I would remember this.

Those fucking assholes.

"You could come back if you agree to my proposition," Ant said, throwing the hilt of the sword between his hands.

My sword forged from the only active volcano across the lands. My sword, the mission that resulted in me losing my damned eye. My sword, the first weapon that had earned me the fury of the gods. The traitor. He threw it between his hands like a worthless stick. That sword didn't belong to him. My growl vibrated loudly, but the frigid wind whisked it away.

"No." I scrunched my hands into fists.

Ant stepped onto the plank, sword out. "No? My cyclone, you aren't in a position to say no."

"No." The edge greeted me.

I gazed at the black water. I swear I could see soft impressions of movement underneath the dark waves. They giggled in velvet, anticipating a feast.

"I just want to share." He waved my sword through the air, weight shifting the plank upwards. I almost fell, my left leg dipping low for balance. The hum of the ocean begged me to slip.

"It's my ship. My crew."

"Only because you stole it from me." Ant winked.

He thought this was funny?

"Should we bring back mortal sacrifices for the merfolk?" Ant said loudly to the crew. His voice dropped. The next words gifted only to me. "C'mon, my cyclone, be reasonable."

Huffing, I looked down. The merfolk would surely enjoy the fresh meat, even from an unwilling meal. I could try to take Ant down with me — he was a bigger meal and potentially a suitable distraction — but I knew his strength and size. It would be a fool's attempt. He had me there. In fact, this was a very similar situation to when I stole the ship from him. Same tricks, a little more clothing. How unimaginative.

If I took a ship again, it wouldn't be the plank that secured my threat. Instead, my attempt would involve feathers and glue.

Ant stepped forward. The plank wobbled.

"Fine!" I grumbled. "Fine, vice-captain. I won't agree to cocaptain, but vice. No more scrubbing the decks."

And with that, Ant sheathed my sword, whipped me up into his arms and walked us back onto the ship. The movement sloppy, but neither of us fell, much to the chagrin of the voiceless merfolk. There would be no free meal today.

"Oh, Captain." He grinned, the scar on the left side of his mouth meeting the crinkles by his eye. "Oh, my captain, I love you so very, very much."

And he kissed me hard, to the jeers of my – our – crew.

The memories distracted as though a reaper burned life before my eye. Despite them, I had made it to the burrow's opening, still alive – for now. The surroundings threatened with wet magic. The burrow, so impossibly circular that it appeared uncanny, looked like nothing more than a trick of my waning mind.

I paused, studying it. The sand shared one shade of orange, with no gradation, as though the magic duplicated itself in each grain, save for the small line of grey that ended at the tip of my toe. I couldn't touch the walls to slip my body through. Instead, I could only leap forward, hands outstretched and ride the dry wave into the Panopticon.

So, I did. The sun let out a final whisper. Night arrived. A full day of travel, welts over my face and hands, far too much water lost through sweat, a bloody ankle, but I finally made it. I clasped my hands and bent my knees. Like a merfolk released from water, I dove through the burrow's black opening and tumbled down.

So, it begins.

2. Level Seven

Pirates colloquially called the Panopticon the seven levels of hell. The worst of the prisons, home to the insane and magic-dealers. It hid completely under dry soil. Despite the respite from the sun and the harsh dry lands, the top level sweltered like air resting on sweating skin.

There was no escape – that was the point of the Panopticon. No trial or sentence, just the promise of suffering. The burrow opened onto the seventh level, and I tumbled arms first, landing in a strategic roll. The slippery slope of the sanded burrow launched me onto concrete ground, the smoothness unnatural against my fingertips after days of nothing but dry sand.

Pain pulsed through my shoulder, but mercifully, nothing seemed broken. Maybe a little bruised, but what was one more wound? Calming my raging breath, I shifted onto my buttocks and looked around.

The colours were an assault on my eye. I blinked heavily. It hurt. Grey and orange. The only two colours, only shades between grey and orange, black and white, red, nothing else. Harsh light illuminated the ceiling, the only fixture above. I saw no sign of the setting sun or of nature's shift in time. Not even the nearby bodies displayed other colours. Prisoners wore grey jumpsuits. The dangerous wore orange. The darker the orange, the worse the prisoner. A legend of the Panopticon, and, as I scanned the curved level, a true one.

My entrance had, of course, caused quite the scene.

I recovered as the prisoners populating the circular level balked at my entrance. The silence built. A woman. Women weren't common prisoners, not here, not in this prison. Only particularly dangerous magic-dealing women were doomed here, but they rarely made it past the sixth level, for many reasons.

Perhaps in another life, I was destined to be a Panopticon prisoner, too.

Instead, I would be its chaos.

The seventh level contained the newest prisoners. Prisoners who'd arrived recently would have lingering strength to fight. The others, however, I looked around, hadn't eaten since Ovators captured them. They wilted, living off tiny water rations and the blood of their fallen cellmates. That's why so many died of toxicity. Liquid became a cruel temptress.

I hadn't seen another mortal in days. Their souls chattered loudly, suffocating in the stale heat.

I didn't know how long they kept prisoners on this level. I pivoted my head, noticing some of the withering, gasping bodies. For some, it could be several weeks. The closest prisoner to me, in a jumpsuit that matched the concrete, curled into himself with closed eyes. He appeared more bone than flesh. Another prisoner besides him scurried away with a bleeding fingertip. He left behind an illustration in the orange clay. His blood barely shone through. The three circles, one small, two encasing it, faded into the nature.

16

Every myth of the Panopticon seemed to hold a little truth. Mostly, however, the inner workings were unknown.

My heart fluttered. Maybe Ant could be on this level.

I shook my head. No, he wasn't. My heart knew it. They wouldn't keep such a powerful pirate as Ant here, for thirst and hunger wouldn't dull his rage. He tugged at my soul, but that tug felt distant.

The level looped as one circular cell as moans and cries died in the curve. No walls divided the space, no privacy, just a slight curve as the circle completed. A structure carved out of dense orange clay. My eye darted across the expanse.

Dozens of prisoners crowded level seven, the space vaster than my limited sight could see. Indeed, it would take much unrecoverable time to traverse it, and that was without threat.

My dagger waited against my hip, my only physical weapon. Most of my trinkets weren't for this fight, but I would be a fool to save them until after my corpse was eaten.

It wasn't the prisoners that troubled me. My eye shifted towards the Guard Tower.

That Central Guard Tower, built in the middle of the prison. An assault of greys. A curved structure, a circular room, the only manmade walls in this entire hellscape. I couldn't see in. I didn't expect to – the windows were thick, dark grey. My reflection almost completely stopped me. A mirror at odds with the myth of the Panopticon. There were no mirrors here, and yet, my reflection greeted me. My headscarf no longer covered my face but wove through the messy raven curls of my long hair, poking out of a loose braid. The dark surface hid most of the damage, and I certainly felt much worse than the reflection conceded. It didn't matter. I waited.

The guards would know.

They watched. They always watched.

Only my reflection stared back.

Several paths led from the Guard Tower to the cell floor, with bits of black nothingness between. Still, no one came out. They invited me to stay, curious, maybe, about this one-eyed pirate who gifted herself to the Panopticon. How far would she go?

All the way.

I stood to my feet, throwing my headscarf to the ground. I would traverse the bottom of hell for even a chance at saving him.

4 DAYS UNTIL CAPTURE:

"There's every chance we'll perish on this adventure." Ant held onto my naked body in our private quarter and though the wooden ceiling camouflaged the night sky, the coolness of the approaching storm soothed me. The ship drifted softly, guided by indulgent waves.

For years, it had been his obsession. His obsession caused his crew to jump captains. At first, I scoffed at the idea, but it had been infectious, and I wasn't immune. His quest for the rhodium sword: the God Killer.

Whilst a volcano imbued my sword with powerful magic, legend told that the God Killer couldn't be forged by mere mortals. Its namesake spoke its truth. The weapon could kill the immortal gods. It waited in the deepest part of the farthest ocean. Many a man had died trying to unearth the God Killer. Many ships decomposed at the bottom of the ocean after facing the wild storms and krakens.

Ant dreamed of change. A dream we'd already spent years pursuing.

Even now he clung to hope as he traced the outlines of raised scars on my skin. Gentle splatters of rain hit the wooden boards outside as thuds in the rhythm of a warning. We were getting closer. The storm was coming.

Ant wanted the God Killer, not to sell it. For surely, he would eventually. It would make us all tremendously wealthy. So ridiculously wealthy, we could even buy land. An actual home on solid land, a land with water and grass. Somewhere for our family.

No, Ant wanted it for revenge.
He wanted to kill a god, the first mortal to do so.

Ant's obsession imprisoned him, for the gods didn't respond kindly
to threats. They never watched, not unless something truly
momentous happened. Not unless something happened to them.
They didn't watch through famines, through plagues, through wars,
in fact, they often created those. But for Ant, they watched. And
for mortals, the loyal, what better way to show faithfulness than to
capture the man who threatened one.

I hated the Ovators. Moreso, I hated the Ovator Guards.

Pious pricks.

I couldn't see the hole down to the next level. The Central
Guard Tower blocked it, the farthest point from the level
above, done so probably to dissuade people like me from going
down. A whole half lap of the level. The prisoners weren't reckless
enough to risk moving down, for every new level posed crueller
threats, execrable pains, until a fate worse than death: level one.

I'm coming, and death better hope to greet me first.

I walked deliberately, careful of the broken prisoners that
surrounded my echoing steps, the movement curing stiffness in my
limbs. My muscles ached from the long journey – arms still tender
from the fall. The air wafted thickly, so impossibly humid. A false
salvation, with no way to harness the air's wetness, the moisture
stolen from prisoners. And now, from me.

At first, the prisoners lining the clay surface just stared at me.
They had nothing to sit on other than the cold, hard concrete.
Some blended with the light grey. Others contrasted in menacing
orange. One boy, barely out of puberty, lifted his hollow gaze
towards me, already splayed as if he no longer accepted movement.
His cheeks were so sunken he looked like a walking corpse. A
skinny hand, arm covered in a light grey jumpsuit, reached out to
touch me. He'd lost three fingers, the nubs a dark maroon, smelling

like death already owned him. A small part of me, a part I'd tried ferociously to kill before coming here, whimpered at his dying form. But he wasn't my mission. His hand dropped, and it brushed against my pant leg. This man posed no threat. Forward, I had to move forward.

The next man who approached me, however, was a threat.

He oozed frantic hunger. His dark grey eyes locked on my blue eye, desire reflecting with such clarity that it stopped me. I existed as a woman in the Panopticon, wearing blue, the mirage of the ocean. His lips smacked together.

The jumpsuit exposed his truth. Light orange, with flecks of grey throughout. He towered with meat still on his bones, but he didn't hold power, and his thirst made him stupid and desperate. I unsheathed my dagger.

The dull brown hilt sat comfortably against my calloused palm. A weapon made with care and precision, but I still missed my sword – the sword I left when Ant stabbed me off our ship. Wherever the sword rested, I prayed it wasn't in the hands of an Ovator. This was Ant's dagger, a gift, and it had taken me a long time to master it. At least my journey provided the time.

I didn't need magic, not here.

The man circled, a performance of a predator. Most people tilted their heads to follow a threat, not me. My one eye strained to look to the right. I whipped my head around.

It had taken months to understand my peripherals, to judge distance accurately. In that time, Ant helped. Despite everything, he helped.

Ant wasn't there when I lost my eye. We met weeks later when I successfully led the commandeer against him, months before we agreed to a tentative alliance as co-captains, years before we sought the God Killer, before we fell in love, when we still learnt each other's dance. When Ant was a prisoner on his own ship.

I had never joined his training before. I was curious, and who could blame me? Ant was magnificent. At first, when I laid eye on the captain of the Blue Abyss, *I saw nothing more than a big, ruthless brute. He had looked so, every inch of him. The shirt he wore looked uncomfortable, like he wasn't a man made for cloth. And the scars. I thought my body bore the marks of a lifetime of fights and challenges, but Ant bore a story in scars, his skin peppered with white and red lightning, the freshest above his heart. He was difficult to look at, difficult to see past the grotesque lines that whispered of destruction. Just like me.*

Ant and I struck a deal. He could train, get precious exercise, for two hours a day, and he would no longer try to escape in the middle of the night and slit my throat.

I locked Ant in the lower deck's cell ever since the night my sinking ship found his. It was after his first escape that I realised he posed more of a threat than his size illustrated. Ruthless, yes, but with an incredible mind, too.

On the first night, he held a knife at my throat as I slept in his former quarters. I opened my eye. We stared at each other for a few moments, the blade cold against my vulnerable flesh.   "Where did you get that?" He pointed to my sword, glowing red, resting above my head.

"Mount Pesorius." My throat bobbed upwards against the icy blade until it no longer pressed against my skin.

The moment sealed me as a better ally than foe. Something about my sword called to him. Curious, the prisoner with the power to make decisions. He took himself back to his cell. It wasn't the last time he put a blade to my throat, but the last time he intended to kill.

So, when he trained, I watched. He moved more delicately than I expected, like a feather, not a stone. And when he offered to train with me, I hesitated at first, then conceded.

It was the only time I allowed the captive out of his prison cell and onto the deck. Of course, my crew — a mix of those faithful only to me and others forced

Ant practically whispered in my ear as I shook my head. This wasn't our ship. The Panopticon, not the ocean, just the grey and orange of my prey.

The prisoner didn't have a weapon, just his size and desperation. He radiated frantic heat.

Ant helped me learn how to shift my movement, how to combat my diminished depth perception, how to exist on the edge of normalcy. It wasn't perfect, but I no longer missed a cup when I poured wine, and I knew exactly how to move my body when the prisoner lunged at me.

The corner of the prisoner's outstretched arm collided with my shoulder. He launched me into the slippery clay wall, the movement offsetting my balance. The prisoner didn't falter. He charged me with chattering teeth. I slid down as determined hands clawed towards my neck, letting the slick wall guide my body before I reached my blade around the prisoner and swiped across his ankle. My blade pierced from one side to the other, ripping apart his ankle's tendon, forcing a slouch. I shifted the blade back to his front and thrust it into his fleshy thigh. He yelped in pain, weighted heavily towards both injuries. Using the injury, I turned the blade with my body, feeling the flesh and muscle give way against the gleaming metal. I rose with the sliding blade. No longer trapped against the wall, I pulled the blade from flesh and slammed it into the side of his neck.

The prisoner had a thick neck. He stood for a moment, as if unwilling to concede to the knife within him. Grey eyes blinked frantically as I carved the few inches of the blade embedded in his artery across the front of his neck, his bobbing throat, and onto the opposite artery, blood spurting from the growing tear. The blade was sharp, but his neck offered resistance against my pull. Blood thickened the air. His mouth fought to make noise, but the gurgles got lost in the wound, vibrating off the circular prison's walls.

He collapsed the moment I freed my blade from his neck.

The other prisoners scavenged as orange and grey jumpsuits who witnessed the fight rushed forward. But they weren't hungry for me. They didn't warm the air for me. No, these were the weakest, most desperate, and there was nothing freer and easier than a fresh corpse.

I retreated, boots leaving bloody prints, watching the frenzy. Several prisoners crowded over the body, teeth and tongues lashing at the fresh blood, still so warm. Tangy urine thickened the air as he relieved what little liquid pooled in his bladder. One prisoner licked the blood pooling below his thigh, unable to get a grip on anything else.

I backed away from the sight, a captured moment of pure desperation. This was the Panopticon, and just the beginning. I peered towards the Central Guard Tower, wondering which of my movements would tempt them out. Nothing. Still no movement.

And yet they watched. They always watched.

I dipped my head. The movement involuntary, my blue eye fierce and steady before continuing around the arched cell. The cell curved so gradually that it proved hard to measure distance. Even the Central Tower was completely cylindrical. The only evidence of progress resonated in the fading sounds of devoured flesh and sipped blood. I looked behind me, mercifully no longer able to see the consequences of my fight, just a fading trail of bloody footprints.

I walked and walked. Despite my waning body, exhausted from the trip so far, I didn't slow. I didn't stop. I grabbed at the zone between my sanity and death, settling there. Moving, walking, forward.

Another prisoner caught my eye, his jumpsuit so light it bordered on cream, splayed on the floor in front of me. Blood trickled down the blade of my dagger as a beckoning on my fingertips. This prisoner was no threat. He waited for death, but I still felt dreadful as I wiped my bloody blade against the leg of his jumpsuit, gifting him a smear of orange. He barely looked at me.

Hesitating, I tapped my belt. The various magic trinkets that lined it weren't yet useful. I couldn't give the man anything as repayment for cleaning my blade. He may deserve to be here – he may not, and who had the right to decide who merited torture in this world? Not even the gods deserved that right.

These men deserved to be freed. There could be nothing they'd done to earn these seven levels of hell, nothing to deserve what awaited them on level one.

I faltered at the next prisoner I passed. He paced. He, in fact, wore a bright orange jumpsuit, a colour that mimicked the setting sun over the desert. With hands clasped behind his back, he walked the same five steps forward, turned, then five steps back. His footsteps echoed off concrete.

It was on his first turn that I noticed why he troubled me so.

He had no eyes. His eye sockets hadn't had time to recover – unlike mine – they were bloody and tender. When a pirate lost an eye, they sought a healer, who sewed the lids shut with dried herbs. It took a few days, but eventually, the lid would press against the socket and the lashes would drop. A funeral for vision. A far too common practice for magic-dealers. The man wasn't gifted the luxury of the procedure.

He still blinked. Blinked. With eyelids. Even with no eyes to moisten. I tried not to stop, not to stare. The prisoner just continued in his holding pattern. I didn't know what he waited for – death, or the next level down. Maybe he no longer wanted, but just existed, stuck in perpetual sorrow. I hovered a hand over my left eye, grateful for it.

I expected more from the Panopticon's top level. More threats, violence, more Ovator Guard presence. The void disturbed me – so many prisoners did little more than sit and wait. Wait until forced down. The reality, however, was much more complex than the concrete floors and orange clay walls divulged. The level's war occurred within the bodies of the prisoners. Thirst and hunger, perhaps an unrelenting dream of freedom juxtaposed with an inescapable knowledge of doom. They were far greater battles to face. No beast or man compared.

I walked, watching as one prisoner bashed his head against the clay wall, his blood congregating in the raised curves of the organic structure. As his neck tilted at my steps, I saw the distinction between blood, flesh and bone, as though the clay imprinted on his forehead like a map. I kept moving.

The hole down to level six approached, signified by the shifting air, the paths to the Central Guard Tower growing more constant, broader. The thickness and humidity plunged closer to that hole. A single, mortal sized circle carved into the concrete. Despite the respite, no prisoners settled nearby, just stifling emptiness. The discomfort of the humidity must've been more palatable than the threats of level six. Only fools sought to go down with free will. The silence warned.

I almost made it, so close to that large, circular void, but faltered. Curiously, the surroundings had remained that deep orange clay. It had become so constant that I couldn't ignore the sudden shift. A pipe gripped against the circular enclosure. I looked longingly at the entrance down but walked closer to the pipe instead. My hand rested in thought atop my curved nose, tapping as though the touch would make sense of the sight.

The clay felt slightly damp, yet firm. The pipe gurgled against my ear. Just one grey pipe reached from the concrete ground, up the clay wall, to the darkened ceiling. A small opening wrapped around the base. Did it go straight through? I tried to move it, shook it. The thing hummed. Was this a water source? I scanned the Panopticon's ceiling, seeing a narrow opening disappear into shadows.

Too high to see. No one could go back up, only down. A truth of the Panopticon, yet I knew of only one entrance. I chewed on my bottom lip, contemplating before shaking the thoughts away. This was a fool's quest. Down, I needed to move down. My body fought against me as I turned around.

Ant is down, not up.

I sheathed my dagger back on my belt. There would be no more threats on this level, but level six was legendary.

I gripped a small canvas pouch on my belt and plucked out a shimmering gold ball, the size of a coin but completely spherical. To the average person, it may appear to be an ornate ball. The shimmering inners moved with the tilt of my fingers in a delicious flurry of seer-blessed metal. A pretty little decoration, but we magic-dealers knew better.

My first trinket, a magic detector. I had brought seven, one for each level and one more for good measure.

The hole betrayed nothing as I hovered above it. It swallowed light. It didn't hint at its threat. I gripped the gold ball between my thumb and pointer finger, fingers already darkened by dried blood, and dropped it.

I waited.

The ball hitting the ground made me groan. As expected, but I really, really hoped it wouldn't be so. Another legend of the Panopticon.

Small wisps of magic-coated brown smoke billowed upwards, daring me to jump down. Of course, I would.

I clenched my fists. Time to tackle the plague.

3. Level Six

1875 DAYS UNTIL CAPTURE:

"They're all dead, Farrah." Ant squeezed my shoulder.

My stare trapped me, the macabre sight a magnet for my eye. An entire village. Thousands of desperately thirsty men, women and children. God's eyes spiced the air, warm and destructive.

We stood on the pier, unwilling to move forward, but unwilling to turn away.

Utorpa was a small village nestled between the dominions of the Fire God and the Wind God. Blessed with the ability to wield and control fire, an enviable place, popular for tourists and land buyers alike. The wind strengthened the flames. Though the land lacked fresh water, it was distinctively small and surrounded by a brilliant turquoise ocean. Villagers boiled, distilled and bottled the water to drink, as well as fed the crops and the abundant green trees. We often traded trinkets for this bottled water.

Sometimes we travelled by sea for months. Bottled water held more value than some of the common magic we dealt in. Perhaps this agreement doomed the village. It had been less than a month since our last visit, and what a cursed month.

Against intuition, we stepped forward.

Most gods forsake their people, leave them to die from plague and illness or no longer bless the crops. But this god still watched. This was wrath.

The village sat in a pile of ashes. Wind blew the fires expeditiously. Although no flames remained, the wind shifted fast and heavy, tickled with that god-touched power. It thickened the air, prickling our skin with dull heat. The villagers had no chance of stopping the firestorm.

It wasn't the wind and fire that killed most, I noticed as my leather boots crunched against charcoaled leaves, but thirst. Bodies lay everywhere, empty, withered, unburnt eyes turned to stone, hair kindling for small wisps of fighting fire.

This bore the mark of the Sea God.

My head thrummed foggily, memories spinning with unwanted frequency as I regained my senses. I didn't crash like I had from the surface to level seven. This time, I calculated my descent, landing on the balls of my feet with knees bent, absorbing the greatest of the impact, but the magic down here throbbed against my brain, swelling to my skull.

Stumbling, I touched my temples. My skull felt intact, my shaky hands roamed across raven hair, but it felt like someone had taken a chisel, carved a hole, and shoved moist cloth between brain and bone.

Level six was legendary. It was, however, rumoured that the plague ruled this level, but this didn't move like the plague. The symptoms gave away its secret. My vision waved and wobbled with brown distortions, and my hearing strained with the undeniable kiss of uncontrolled magic. It prickled at my brain, seeking entry, seeking to invade. My hands shook as I clawed at my belt, motions limited by pure, sickly sweet magic.

How ridiculous. Magic here – in the Panopticon.

I was prepared for it, but I didn't miss the irony.

Mercifully, I had packed a small bag of medicines. I undid the drawstrings of a velvet pouch tucked on my belt. My hands faltered, eye strained to differentiate between the red pill and the brown pill, definitely not the two black pills, until I saw that little yellow pill tucked in the bottom corner. I blinked. My fingers missed it, grasping at air before settling on rough velvet. Furrowing my brows, I concentrated on nothing more than the hinging of fingers, the pressure as they touched the little yellow pill. It felt cold and coarse. My fingers wobbled under strain, uncertain I could carry its weight.

I got it. I fumbled the pill into my mouth, lingering on my tongue, waiting anxious moments for my brain to force a swallow.

My throat burned as the pill fought gravity, grazing my dry throat the whole way down. I ignored the light-grey pipe that threatened the corner of my eye. It would have to wait.

I still knelt, allowing myself to curl over, unable to absorb my surroundings, unable to fight anything that challenged the woman with one eye who imposed on this level. Breathe. It was all I could do. Breathe slowly, breathe and let the pill work. The magic burst through my mind like sprouting seeds, and I waited for the yellow pill to dull the intrusions. Time waned.

Was it an aeon before my strength rose enough to look around, or mere seconds? Time, importantly, didn't move linearly here. Bodies still withered from thirst and hunger, but time didn't shift the same as on the surface. The sun didn't rise. No day, no night. It stagnated. It didn't flow, not like it should. Not an ocean, but a bog instead.

1875 DAYS UNTIL CAPTURE:

"We don't have time," Ant said.

He was right, but I couldn't leave her. She was one girl. One girl who'd survived the wrath of three gods. One girl who endured the thirst, the fires and the wind. She would surely perish here, another corpse feeding the village's dirt. Perhaps we should've let her. But we owed this place we doomed with our trading. Maybe the gods didn't like the abundance of trade this village conducted with magic-dealers. Maybe the gods just didn't like us. Or, more accurately, didn't like me.

One girl, who now stood at the base of the charcoaled boardwalk, adorned in silky white robes, as our ship slowly drifted away. Most mortals would've faded against the charcoal leaves and decrepit dwellings. But not her. Her silver hair glistened, the only light in the desolate darkness. Curious, I had never seen such a unique shade, not on someone so young. The sky above thickened with gods' eyes. They threatened, but no, we had to help. We had to turn back. The gods didn't own her death.

The girl would eventually grumble at being called this. She was a woman, so she'd bark.

She wasn't. A teenager, maybe fifteen or sixteen, she didn't know her exact age, and looked so frail and malnourished, it was hard to tell. She didn't have a family, sold young to a rich Ovator, mansion proudly perched on the steepest

Navira, mercifully, didn't sail with us to the God Killer, nor when the Ovators swarmed our ship so close to shore. Wherever she was now, I could only hope we'd prepared her for the ferocity of the world and the gods. I suppressed the gnawing guilt at abandoning her. We'd been a family. Family distracted.

Finally, I raised my head, banishing the thoughts. Control returned, ever so slightly. Perspiration clung to my long raven hair, running down my neck, wetness far too great for only level six. My braid hugged wet skin, salty sweat burning into the boils and welts endowed by the oppressive desert sun. There must be water somewhere. There must be some source that kept prisoners from completely perishing. Mother, I needed it.

The grey and orange surroundings wore a brown hue. Everything appeared a little darker, nothing shone white. My hand reached out to grasp the air, small speckles of that brown magic coating like a thin dust. It chased my fingers, working to claim every inch of skin, but I couldn't feel it. If I narrowed my eye enough, I could see the miniscule particles laced with magic, and the spaces between free of its grasp. It smelled of stale earth.

I glanced at the Central Guard Tower, an exact replica of the previous floor. No movement, the same dark grey reflective surface, though dimmed by the magic hue.

Yet I knew they watched. They always watched.

The Ovator Guards were nothing but hypocrites. Magic wielding and selling was the crime of at least half the prisoners within these circular walls, and yet it ruled this level.

Curious, was it meant to subdue its subjects? I looked around. The jumpsuits leaned more orange than grey, as though magic culled the weak, but a gradation remained.

Space restricted, clay walls pulsed as though ready to collapse, and the level brimmed with fullness. Not with prisoners, but with everything else. Despite the magic dust that fogged my distant vision, this floor appeared more permanent. Cots hugged the walls of the Panopticon. Small, the thinnest cotton fabric, and comfortable only for the slightest of bodies. I tried not to imagine Antorn sprawled across one, feet dangling through brown dust. Two metal rods held the cots together, the fabric grazing the ground with the heaviness of sleeping bodies. The dormancy was as confronting as level seven's desperation.

I found the lightest, greyest jumpsuit I could decipher. An ageing man with a thick white beard and peeling skin sat at the edge of a cot, legs tapping against the concrete floor in a constant rhythm. He stared at me curiously with a withering gaze.

"You!" I pointed as I walked towards him, my other hand at the hilt of my dagger.

He didn't respond. He was lucid enough – his eyes shifted, understanding painted his face as his gaze travelled from boots to braid. It was when his eyes met my one, when they widened at the ocean that looked back at him, that I gripped my dagger and released it from its hilt.

"Is there water?" I pointed my blade toward his chest.

The man didn't move, just continued rustling, swaying his legs backwards and forwards, tap, tap. A painfully melodic sound.

I considered asking a different prisoner. The pill worked, taking the edge off the airborne magic poison, but my thoughts still jumbled, my hands still struggled to comply with the commands of my mind. I had to think the thoughts and will them into action.

Turn around.

Finally, the man said, "The only water here is the ocean you wear."

I blinked. *Turn around,* I instructed my body. Instead, I stared.

"I do not wear the ocean." My voice rang hoarse and dry. "It's the colour of my eye."

"It is not your eye." The man stared at my empty eye socket. "You carry the ocean."

The man paused a beat. He continued swaying, tap, tap. He opened his mouth once more.

"But I do not know if you will doom us or save us all."

I stepped back. Was it a threat? I needed to turn. Most pirates knew to thwart threats, most pirates didn't let words sit uncontested. Even in here, the Panopticon, I should slit the man's throat for whispering blue words. Threats should be challenged – it was the pirate way.

It was when Ant challenged a threat, not against me but Navira, that I first told him I loved him too. The memory clawed to the front of my mind.

1782 DAYS UNTIL CAPTURE:

"Where is she?"

I never let panic shine through my words, never let fear project on my face, tremble through my hands. But Navira hadn't come back to the ship that night, and my body betrayed me. I shook, though the air warmed. The sky abandoned light, the moon little more than a promise behind plush clouds. Nothing good happened at this hour.

A storm had passed, leaving the ground wet and puddled. The air hung with wisps of lingering power.

She'd been with us for a few months, and within that time, Ant and I had gotten much closer to each other, and much closer to Navira. She was a curious girl. Headstrong, despite being born into a life of unfortunate suffering. And yet, she stared at the stars as if they still answered prayers. A dreamer gifted a childhood of nightmares.

This sheer dumb optimism veiled the real world's truth from her eyes. Optimism blinded her to the jeers of the desperate, drunk men. Navira had barely started training, still frail and weak, despite the curves of her body. The curves that attracted the stares, as well as the curious silver shade of her hair, like liquid metal. She was safe with Ant and me, but she promised she'd return. A stupid, feckless teenager. One drink, just one drink, one ale in a big, busy tavern. What could happen? She had begged. Hours ago, now. She longed for company, for those of her age. She hadn't returned.

We soon realised teenagers shouldn't be trusted with liquor.

Ant charged first as we stormed the barn after the bartender barked her location between choked breaths. Let him go, *I said to Ant,* we need to hear what he says before he dies. *I didn't care about the bartender's life. I cared for few lives, all of which rested on that ship of ours*

Navira wore that indulgent cotton gown, the first dress we had bought her. She dyed it powder blue, spending all her coins on the azurite pigment. Impractical on a ship, but we didn't care. She wanted to wear a dress because she claimed it was her birthday. A pretty blue dress to mark a date she fabricated as special. But it had been pushed upwards. The man pinned her against the wall. She wore dirt and hay and sweat, her hair a dull grey, rather than shining silver, sickly ale fighting the barn's strong manure scent.

We arrived in time, but we had little left. Ant moved fast, faster than his size implied. He reached the man — wearing that mark, the flesh dealer's mark — turned him, and shoved a knife straight through his eye. The man choked on a scream. The action was too quick, too merciful. His blade pierced through eye, then bone and, finally, brain. His heart would beat to a brainless mind, at least for a few more moments. A nameless man gifted with a swift death.

Too swift.

Navira trembled, pressed against the wall, knuckles whitening as if her flesh yearned to turn to stone. She said nothing as the man's body collapsed to the ground. She looked as she was — a caged pet, finally released to a vicious, unrelenting land. Perhaps now, despite everything, she yearned to return to the torture she knew.

She was safe. I gripped her, pushing her towards the barn door before anyone questioned the commotion. We had to go. Ant said nothing as he took the blade from the man's skull and sheathed it, but his hands shook.

"I love you too." I clutched his shirt in my fist, gazing deeply into that determined golden-brown gaze. The truth sailed on my lips for months, finally released. I loved him.

He looked irate, but I knew the truth. He trembled, chest heaving. Fear grasped Antorn. He didn't want to lose her. Neither did I.

My words permeated his haze, shattering his mind's barrier.

His eyes found me, softening.

The three of us never spoke about it again.

But this man, this prisoner, he didn't threaten me, not like the man threatened Navira in the barn. After years on the ocean, after stories of fights and pain were written on my body in the language of scars, wisdom became difficult to identify. Everything burned like opposition.

"Thank you, but I won't doom us." I thought of Navira and Antorn.

"Why are you here?" he asked with a scratchy voice.

He tried to look at me, but the gaze only lasted a second. His eyes fought to stay upward, drifting to the ground as though propelled by an invisible force. Just like my body didn't want to obey commands, his didn't want to hold a gaze. And what a tragedy. His eyes were a wonderful shade of brown, like mud that coated the feet of giggling children. Whatever life he lived suffocated in brown magic, and I couldn't revive him.

This man didn't have medicine. He lived through the magic poison that dulled him. His body perhaps adapted slowly, but how long until Ovator Guards dragged him down a level? Forced to face a different, greater threat? What level earned his death?

"I wish to burn the place down," I said.

While somewhat true, my mission would end in one of two ways: I would either fail alone, or I'd take the whole goddamn Panopticon with me.

"Drown it," he whispered.

His gaze no longer reached mine. His body remained, but mind disappeared in thick brown mist.

I had to walk. Distance seemed greater down here, and I was so tired. How long had I been awake? How long without food and water? The prisoners on this level behaved docile, infected with the magic poison. They strained at movement, fighting against their body's desire to shut down completely. My body willed itself to move and breathe, awakened by medicine, but for the rest of them, those actions were like climbing up to the top of a mountain, only to fall on jagged cliff edges.

The thirst built. My eye darted from left to right, body turning to capture what my sight missed. Only prisoners lay on those cots. No food, no water, nothing to quench what burned in me. I reminded myself to breathe, to swallow a large bite of air and let it out. Again, and again, and again. Mother, I was thirsty.

One prisoner in a pale orange jumpsuit, slender with a soft round face, lunged at me, coated in a brown fog. His body acted separate to his mind, and he leaped so pathetically that his forehead collided with concrete. His hands forgot to stop the force. I didn't have to lift his head to see the crack in the frontal bone. A crunch told me the prisoner was dead. Brown magic fled his soulless corpse as his last heartbeat failed him.

The magic didn't flow constantly throughout this level but comigrated in sections of the curved structure. It gathered around the deteriorating prisoners squatting on cots as though they were feeding stock, prisoners who kept the magic alive, the magic that kept them meek.

What a vicious cycle. Magic living off the suffering of prisoners.

My feet protested forward movement, begging to stop. I had to move quick, resist the temptation to slow down, to rest, to pause.

Empty cots lay tempting against the clay wall. No prisoners. One section, reserved for the ghosts of prisoners, enticed me. I could rest, sheltered in the thick brown magical dust, perhaps regain my waning energy. My body yearned for rest, but if I rested, the pill would wear off, and I brought no other.

No, I kept moving.

I could sleep when I was dead.

My tapping boots against concrete filled the barren space, echoing as evidence of progress. Fewer prisoners settled the further I walked. I pondered this as I rounded another slight curve of the circular level. Maybe half of the previous one. Perhaps the magic took the weakest, perhaps that was why orange jumpsuits triumphed over shades of grey.

Perhaps the weakest just forgot to breathe. The thought rested contentedly at my core, for that was a peaceful death, and hell wasn't known for peace.

I willed myself to swing and face the Central Guard Tower. It sat mostly outside my peripheral vision. It hummed.

They watched. They always watched.

And yet, they didn't stop me. They did nothing as I rounded another slight curve and saw the hole down. That perfectly circular entrance. Level five, I had made it.

My hand had numbed so much, it built to a paralysing ache. It stung to grip the canvas pouch of shimmering gold balls and pluck one out. My fingers warmed uncomfortably.

The next magic detector. Invisible needles lay between the magic of the ornate ball and my fingers, fighting against the brown magic dust that followed me, even though it dwindled towards the entrance down.

I hovered the magic detector above the blackness. Once more, I could see nothing within, just darkness and foreboding. Going down opposed every bit of intuition, and that feeling built with every level, every threat. The Panopticon was a circular maze of torture, and I willed myself through it.

The ball dropped, a little clink as it hit the bottom. Nothing, no billow of smoke, no indication of magic. Whatever magic touched level six didn't reach the one below. In fact, the magic hovered above the hole as if it dared not mix with the rival air.

The brown magic feared it – not a good sign.

I sighed as I rolled my shoulders, fastening the canvas pouch to my belt. No magic should be a good sign, so why did it make my blood curdle?

I swung my legs through the hole and fell to level five.

The legends were wrong.

This was the plague.

4. Level Five

The plague's odour hit my lungs as an instant warning. Without windows, without fresh air, it stagnated. I landed on the balls of my feet once more, knees forward, taking the brunt of my descent in a body stronger than the last time I faced the plague.

It had been almost two decades since that smell filled every crevice of my nose, when I still had two eyes, when I first learnt how to walk alone. Before my skin told any story. And yet, I recognised it as if it were yesterday.

7117 DAYS UNTIL CAPTURE:

I was just a girl. A similar age to Navira when Ant and I found her. My skin silken and untouched. It was a month until I'd marry, and I was elated to be betrothed to a beautiful, golden-haired boy. He was simple, meek and perfect — my only dream in my small existence.

It wasn't fated, not meant to be. The gods didn't want the union, and I didn't understand why. They surely would regret unleashing me.

The plague moved slowly, not like fire or flood, but spread strategically in waves that made little sense. My father died first. He'd secured my betrothal at a young age, even bartered for the arrangement to start two full years after my first bleeding. He was the strongest of us. And yet, the weakest.

The fever came first. We had to change the sheets nightly, for the dampness brought forth the black mould, and the black mould brought forth the plague. After a few weeks, when his condition worsened, when his vomit ran no longer brown and thick but red and thin, we no longer kept him in the bed but the tub. His body ached regardless of what we did, even the softest pillows our meagre savings could buy felt like knives against his peeling skin. The hard tin tub barely registered as distinctive.

He rested there until speech failed him, until his breaths were so shallow, they never satisfied. I always thought about that — how painful it must be to fail at breathing, to never pull a satisfying breath, to never feel full lungs. It made me grateful for my own breath, but so fearful that it too would stop.

My mother died next, then my brother, then my sister, then my betrothed. The plague ravaged my entire village. It smelled horrible — like damp old rotting meat.

I had no choice but to leave before the plague took me. It took weeks to reach the ocean, but that was when I relinquished my title of small-village girl with hope for a small love, to pirate. I joined the first ship willing to take on an inexperienced girl. The first touch of salty sea air on my skin hooked me. The first time my fingers glided over turquoise water, I understood love.

Now and then, that scent revisited my nightmares.

I glanced first at the Central Guard Tower, my reflection clear without the fog of brown magic, like a lifted veil. Desperate determination stared back. That girl, who had wanted to live a small life, wanted an insignificant love, had died. Died, probably at

40

least five stab wounds ago, maybe six, if that one counted. I nursed my backside. My blue eye shone boldly down here, truly endangered, difficult to ignore. I narrowed it, willing for the Ovator Guards to come out, to fight me.

But they didn't.

They watched. They always watched.

The unmistakable scent of wet rotting meat filled my nostrils. It wasn't like my village, where the scent lingered on the infected, but could be escaped by the fresh outdoor wind. No, it staled without relief. It may be too late, but I had prepared for this. The legend of the Panopticon Plague infected the nightmares of all magic-dealers.

An inescapable plague. A waiting game, unknowing whether a body would fight or succumb. Inescapable to a prisoner, but not to an uninvited guest.

The leather mask wasn't secured on my belt, but against my breasts. I stuck a hand down my tunic and grasped at the mask, pulling it out from between bindings and flesh. It dripped with sweat. Leather wasn't the wisest material to have against flesh, particularly when traversing an entire desert, but if the rumours of the plague rang true, the beaked mask would help.

The mask was custom made to fit my face. It instantly overwhelmed. Stifling, the surroundings crept tightly, pressed with leather and glass. Only one crystal lens was used in the design so my eye could see, but thick rims of black lining limited my sight. The mouth beaked long and protruded so that my breath could move, but it was thick and heavy. Despite this, it protected me. I had worn this mask, trained in it. Although a limit to my sight, the mask could shield from infection.

Level five was a frenzy. Prisoners crowded the space. Thin cotton cots still surrounded the orange clay walls, but many were torn and ripped.

The first prisoner I saw was dead. He lay limply in front of me, grey jumpsuit, hand still clasping torn cotton. Eyes brown, glazed and lifeless, frozen in shock, as if death arrived unexpectedly. No blood pooled, no sweat – not a plague victim. I walked to his left, my eye not used to the black outline framing the prison. I stared down at him, his throat black and compressed. Someone had collapsed his windpipe as they strangled him. I motioned to touch the body, to gather how long it had been here, but reconsidered.

This wasn't a level to linger on, or a death to care for. It was too late, and whatever had threatened him remained. I unsheathed my dagger and gripped it tightly.

The thirst within me grew with the confining, uncomfortable restrictions of the leather mask. It stuck to my damp forehead, restricting my breathing. I had to find water. This level must have some. There had been none on the previous two, but there must be some here. My throat bobbed dry as I gulped down sand, not saliva. Every part of my being wanted to rip the mask off, but not yet. The plague moved quickly, even more so with the way time stagnated within the Panopticon. Perhaps days had already passed, perhaps only minutes. Time didn't control the plague – there was no wave.

I found the first awake prisoner on the level, despite the deep orange of his jumpsuit, and pointed my dagger straight at him. He wandered the walkway, the only purpose in his miserable existence.

"You!" The mask muffled my voice. "Is there anything to drink on this level?"

The prisoner didn't wear a mask. He was infected, with exposed skin matching the shade of his jumpsuit, covered in colourful bruises. It was the closest to purple I had seen in the Panopticon, and it shimmered with the sweat that dripped from his open pores. His bruises didn't dare shine green. It almost made me pause.

"Yes." His voice weak, edged with something more. "Right here."

He pointed down to his crotch. I suppressed the urge to stab it.

"My qualm is not with you," I said, words flat. "So, I ask again, where is the water?"

The prisoner unzipped his jumpsuit, the zip lining from his chest to his stomach. I shifted my weight from one leg to the other. The jumpsuit fell to his ankles. He was naked, bruises splotched across his body, bones protruding from thin skin, staring at me with shallow brown eyes and a hollow smirk. It was absurd.

"Sir." My voice grew louder. "If you do not dress, I will cut your penis off."

This didn't get the response I wanted. He urinated, scrunching his nose. The thickness of the mask shielded me from the unpleasant scent, but beneath the leather, I grimaced.

So, I made good on my word. Then I stabbed him in the heart for good measure.

I pondered whether the man deserved to die as I wiped his blood on his jumpsuit. Crimson blended with orange. He was, after all, offering me a form of liquid, but the plague tainted his urine, and it flowed thick and brown. It would offer no one hydration, and for the indecency he thrust on my eye, he deserved to die.

The first time I saw Ant naked was a very different experience. The memory consumed my thoughts.

2101 DAYS UNTIL CAPTURE:

I had spent over a decade working my way up the ranks on various ships. I told myself I had escaped the plague, but illness and destruction seemed to infect the islands. The sea, however, held escape. I worked on small ships, then medium, then big. At first, I scrubbed the decks, then commanded the sails, before being promoted to boatswain. My very first adventure as captain, captain of a meagre crew of six, didn't go well.

Our ship was sinking, that was clear. We'd just successfully forged my sword in the lava of Mount Pesorius. That sword, however, wouldn't save the ship from a wrathful storm. A storm designed to tease a slow, drowning death. Mercifully, we'd spotted another ship in the middle of the ocean, quietly sailing without a care in the world. A ship much bigger, much newer, much better kept.

We had a choice. I had a choice. Go down with this ship or commandeer that one. Barely a choice.

The sea had flooded our deck by the time a wave bumped us against the lacquered hull of the enemy ship. The water welled around my legs like tar. I didn't hesitate as my navigator flung a rope, catching it around a cannon. We crept upwards, me first, me and my precious sword.

My vision suffered at night. The one eye made it difficult to decipher changes in environments, and I still mourned my old sight.

But when we rose to the top, falling onto the deck, good fortune greeted us with a passionate embrace.

This ship held a similar number of pirates, maybe one or two more. Such a small crew for such a big ship. Not enough to outnumber us, certainly not now. They were all drunk, sitting in a circle, all naked.

My navigator, Daphne, couldn't help but stare at the dangling penises. I gave her a pointed look. Keep your sword raised high, unlike the men.

They played cards. The thick scent of wheat and barley unmasked the casual nature of the night. Every single pirate looked at us, a few gawking from underneath spilling mugs. Of course, being naked, they were without weapons.

"Who is your captain?" My voice shook a little.

"That would be me." A big man stood. "Antorn, Captain of the Blue Abyss.*"*

He strode over to me, completely ignoring the sword pointed at his chest until it touched him, right where brown thread hugged a large, purple mark.

This man was immense. Immense in every sense of the word. I tried not to blush. This was the type of man my parents warned me about. A stupid, dangerous pirate. But I was one, too. The small village girl died, and what survived was a harsh, vicious woman, already marred by the lines of danger a pirate life gifted. He didn't scare me. I intended to scare him.

He stood a startling contrast of muscle, scars and beautiful silky brown hair. Only his large, pointed nose could stop me from reading the scars lining his mouth. His uniqueness hesitated me, but I was desperate, pragmatic.

The Panopticon played tricks on my memory, my sense of linear time. Life flashed in inexplicable fragments, memories willing me forward. I was too thirsty, too drained. I moved several paces from the fallen prisoner when the next intrusion struck me.

Despite its necessity, the mask was a terrible idea. The movement of the prisoner – who grabbed my shoulder and slammed us onto the ground – rested completely outside my scope of vision. Thankfully, he hadn't been smart. The prisoner was ravenous, gripped by disease and illusion. He pulled me backwards, and I landed on flesh, stealing his breath with my descent. Despite my advantage, bony, desperate hands clawed at me, feeling mostly cotton, but tearing skin at my neck and clavicle. I screeched, the skin burned raw with the boils of the sun, the cuts like hot metal poured onto open wounds.

I tried to wiggle off the prisoner, but my body struggled with the uneven weight. Shifting onto my side, I offset the curve of my spine, flipping towards the ground. My blade rested in my hand, and I gripped it tighter. My only weapon – the only weapon in this entire cell. The mask completely obscured my vision of him, hidden in shadowed blackness. I rolled to the right, seeing only the Central Guard Tower.

They watched. They always watched.

Perhaps this was when they hoped to see my end.

They wouldn't.

In one swift move, I flung onto my buttocks and slid, just in time to see the prisoner lunge downwards at me.

Death, so much death here.

He met my blade. It didn't quite pierce his heart. It entered low, right between his fourth and fifth ribs. But he had plenty of organs, veins, and tendons, and could still feel pain, even through the fever's obfuscation. He squealed, a sound not too dissimilar to the one I let out as he scratched me, like a seeking twin.

He rested embedded on the end of my blade, his hands grasping the hilt to unravel, but I held on. I studied his face – the fever had gotten him. He dripped salted sweat, pattering like rain onto my mask. I pushed, I turned. I used all my strength to shift the prisoner forward, kneeling as he slumped to the ground. He would bleed out slowly, and he would see my masked face as he died. The bringer of death.

With mercy, I pulled the blade out and plunged it into his heart.

Another mind my mission destroyed. Another soul that may or may not deserve it. But I'd told myself before starting this journey that they were better off dead than suffering. My blade was a mercy in a place like this. A few coughs echoed off the circular prison design, but no one approached the corpse. No one dared. With the mask, I avowed death, and in the Panopticon, death was inevitable.

Yet the prisoners seemed desperate to cling to life.

Ant had introduced me to tales of the Panopticon the first night I commandeered his ship and locked him in the cell. My first prisoner.

2101 DAYS UNTIL CAPTURE:

After being forced on the plank and conceding his ship, Antorn requested clothing, to which I showed mercy. He stood in the holding cell. In fact, he had to tell me how to get there, being his ship. It was very odd, leading a prisoner down, pressing a sword against his bare back, asking whether it was to the left or right. The cell glowed pristine, lacking the signs of omnipotent haunting I required to truly complete this takeover as a fearful pirate.

Once the lock clicked shut, I faltered. It was my most successful, most aggressive takeover. I had done it. I'd saved my crew. And yet, now I imprisoned someone. What did that make me? Was I no better than—

"It is no Panopticon." Antorn laughed as if sensing my hesitation, his forearm resting against the cold grey bars as he leaned carelessly. "I will be fine."

"I'm not worried," I spat back before adding, "What's the Panopticon?"

He pulled on black leather pants but hadn't put on a top. He had muscles and scars. It was hard to differentiate which part of his raised body was muscle and which was tissue. It was frightening. And yet, as he leaned against the cell door, I admired the story his body told. For my body revealed a similar novel, and it was only later that I realised we were a pair in a greater story. An incomplete duology.

He laughed once more, but his beautiful golden-brown eyes silvered. "The Panopticon is death. But slower."

"Yes, but what is it?" I didn't have time for legends.

"It's a prison governed by the Ovators to appease their gods, a terrible place filled with famine and disease and violence. No one leaves. There is no trial, only punishment. No one escapes. Legend has it that the very bottom holds a rare form of god magic."

"If no one escapes, how do you know what it is?"

Ant shrugged as he lowered his arm. "Legends are stronger than mortality."

I considered, then turned.

"What can I call you, my captor?" Antorn asked.

"Farrah," I spoke softly back.

"Farrah, the Cyclone of the Seas."

Hunger and exhaustion triumphed over my memories. My mask stuck to my skin as a constricting, suffocating layer. I tugged at it to give some respite, but it just clung back as soon as my fingers let go of the thick leather. I contemplated throwing the damn thing on the ground and just getting on with it, but one look around the level stopped me.

Death controlled the level like its conqueror. So many bodies lingered on its cusp, and those who didn't attack me tried to watch.

They failed. Their life failed them. The smell… the smell thinned, with only a negligible amount of rotten wet carcass breaching the mask. Orange and grey jumpsuits darkened with sweat, urine and faeces. Fever fought many as I passed their cots, the coughs sending a shiver down my spine.

Some cots rested as skeletons without flesh. Metal rods holding emptiness. Cotton sat folded in a perfect circle, but there was nowhere to hang it. The roof was too high to reach, impossible to breach to the level above, and the roof remained smooth grey concrete, except for a few bright bulbs.

A prisoner may have introduced the plague, or nature or the gods may have intervened. However it got here, the plague now controlled it. The prisoners, its victims.

I walked until I caught an unmistakable glisten of wetness. My throat bobbed, mouth watering with anticipation.

There, in the curve of the clay walls, in the hands of a freshly deceased corpse, sat a wet ball of cotton.

I looked around, steadying my pace. Any prisoner who understood what drew me would surely contest the find. Surely my thundering heart gave it away. Surely it was all anyone could hear. It bellowed so loudly within the mask, so deafening.

The prisoner hadn't been dead long. It could've been minutes since he'd taken his last breath, and he showed no signs of stiffness. I didn't care. So, this was how they hydrated. The little cotton ball sat wet in his open hand, as if a gift in death. I snatched it in one swift motion, feeling the water leak into the pores of my palm.

Hands shaking, I pulled the edge of my mask upwards and fed through the cotton ball, so it rested below my nose. I sniffed. Nothing, just scentless water. Before I could hesitate, before I could rethink the risks of infection, the wet ball fell in my mouth.

The noise that escaped me told a melody of immortal joy. I had known pleasure, but no pleasure like this. The fabric gushed water that coated my mouth, enough to swallow.

Just one gulp.

I didn't dare fish the cotton from my mouth, pushing it across my teeth, my gums, my tongue. Every molecule within that cotton ball needed to be consumed. I moved with it, feeling a little more optimistic as I continued forward.

That cotton ball of water may have saved me. The death of that prisoner may have saved me.

Thank you, I whispered to his ghost as I continued forward, hoping his next life offered more peace.

The prisoners posed a minimal threat. They fought their own battles with illness. Even the darkest orange jumpsuits didn't bother me. Yes, I was a woman, but with the mask, I resembled a reaper. They just stared and watched, waiting. Maybe some of them knew I was no threat. Those lucid enough, those not driven insane by the fever.

Only one more man tried to contest me. He even reached for the golden monocular fastened around my belt, but he too was slow and dying. Now, he was dead. Another nameless victim of the plague, left with nothing more than a colour. I tried not to think of him. I had to move forward.

There, in front of me, swirling, circular blackness. The hole signalled the next level down. Ant told me about this level too, on one of those precious nights under the stars where he bared his soul.

The middle level.

The great equaliser. I didn't know where he had learned these myths. His father had been a Panopticon prisoner but hadn't survived. No one did. So, where did the myths come from?

He never told me why the fourth level haunted him the most. It baffled me since he knew what rested on level one… what now waited steadily for him. This memory – the fear leaking from his words that night – spurred my need to rescue him. Fate couldn't repeat. His father didn't have a Farrah. Antorn did.

The same pipe rested in my peripheral vision, the same grey pipe, still inaccessible, still unusual. This level, however, wet with plague, reminded me that there wasn't time to investigate further. I had to move on. The mask wouldn't protect me forever, not from every microscopic disease particle that swarmed the air, seeking a host.

I fished another small golden ball out of the canvas pouch and placed it in the swirling, darkened black hole. The hole down. A perfect circle, in a perfectly circular Panopticon.

It fell in. The smoke wafting up was as crimson as the blood drying on my knife.

Fuck.

5. Level Four

Red smoke wasn't good. Brown, sure, brown could be a problem. Brown magic infected its victims severely. But magic that left a red hue? It was unpredictable, uncontrollable – the colour of unruly power.

Prisoners attacked me the instant my feet touched the fourth level. They barrelled into me, heated and desperate. My masked skull smacked against the concrete ground.

The starvation occurred on level seven, poison on level six, and plague on level five. The magic here reinvigorated anyone from the cusp of death. It gave dumb, desperate and dying men a stupid belief in their waning strength. Their stupidity echoed through fiendish growls.

Flashes of blood orange grabbed at me. My neck still pulsed raw from the scratches, skin still boiling from the sun. My arms and legs were being stretched, a pair of incessant hands on each limb. I heard a pop, then a sharp pain flew up my shoulder. Not the worst pain, and I had experienced many, many types of pain. Being stabbed being one of the worst, depending on the location of the wound.

It wasn't the first time I'd been stabbed that flooded my mind as though death recited my life's story. No, but the first time because of Ant. The deep scar rested on my thigh, mere inches from my femoral artery.

220 DAYS UNTIL CAPTURE:

"She fucking stabbed me!"

And she did. Ant's ex-lover turned out to be a former betrothed, and she hadn't moved on from the tryst. For some unknown reason, she felt it more appropriate to stab me than stab him.

We were enjoying a ritualistic ale in a nameless town's tavern when the woman approached with fury in her grey eyes. The tavern was dim, wooden brown, painted by shadows, a little wet with ale and sweat, and a complete copy of all the other taverns that lined the magic trading route. A simple place, unassuming, filled with richness in its stories rather than décor.

"You're alright." Ant's eyebrows furrowed as he looked down at the blade still embedded in my thigh. "It missed your artery."

"Oh, what a relief." My crimson cheeks matched the blood dripping from my thigh. "You need to kill her."

Ant didn't respond at first, his eyes fixed on the blade. He placed a hand on the hilt and cowered at the moan of pain that escaped my lips. He wanted to grip the dagger and pull it out, but it was in a dangerous spot, and any wrong move and I would become a bloody tap.

"Did you hear me, Ant?" I growled. "If it were a man that stabbed me, you would kill him."

Ant rose, the tavern thick with an awkward tension that bounced off its walls as a summons for more violence. Fights weren't unusual around the pirate taverns, but my reaction had caused quite the spectacle. I noticed, adding to my embarrassment and anger, that they seemed more entertained than concerned. Everyone listened, taking deep swigs of beer.

"I hear you." He wore a cheeky grin, though his eyes betrayed his worry. "And call me sexist, my cyclone, but I will not kill her. Plus, she's already long gone."

He motioned towards the door, which slammed shut as the woman exited after realising her folly. Ant didn't scare her. No, she still loved him. Even with a dagger in my thigh, she was petrified of me.

She fucking should be.

"Let's get you to a healer." He motioned to pull me up, but I swatted his hand away.

"I can move myself."

It took all my energy to shuffle out of there with my head held artificially high and a blade poking out of my thigh. Ant let me.

Limping in pain, I realised that whilst Ant was my first real love, I had not been his.

And yet, what woman was being stretched and mutilated on level four of the Panopticon just to rescue him? Where was that other bitch now?

The thought of that stab awakened something primal inside me. Four prisoners surrounded like predators, clawing at me, without purpose, without direction. Even though my mask muffled their sounds, they barked like beasts. One had grabbed my dagger and carved delicate lines into my calf. My shoulder had popped out of place. Mercifully, that was the worst of the damage. I still wore the plague mask, and that may have kept me alive. At least, what kept my eye safe.

With my free right arm, the one still firmly within its socket, I fumbled against my belt until my hands gripped something soft and plush. The magic trinket wasn't meant for the men of this level, but it would do me no good if I were already dead.

This magic trinket cost Ant and me almost a year's worth of treasures. It felt like a stupid purchase. Trinkets were like precious jewels – some more common than others. Ant certainly loved collecting rare trinkets more than he loved sailing the seas. We were opposite, in that regard. I sought magic trinkets for the freedom of the ocean, the contrast of the blistering sun and icy blue water. Ant sailed towards an end, a way to get magic. A way to get revenge.

I almost didn't squeeze down on the soft trinket, glowing a gorgeous, shifting yellow, gleaming as though I watched the sun sparkle from another planet. I was perhaps better off dead than wasting the one use this soft ball had. A shame to waste on the prisoners of this level, even though it may save my life. No time to dwell. My body stretched, shoulder dislocated, leg mutilated, and my mask could only protect me for so long. I thumbed the furry outside of the ball until my finger felt that hidden little trigger. My index finger stretched until it landed on the second trigger. The magic shuddered against my fingers, my palm, until I pushed down with all my might. I squeezed my eye closed.

The violent white light that surrounded us blinded, unleashing bottled starlight. It emitted a shrill, high-pitched scream. Even with the mask, even with my obscured vision, the crystal lens, my eyelid, the pain shot through my eye and sent lightning through my skull. The trinket destroyed colour with light until time forced it back. The flash startled the prisoners. Two died in an instant, killed by the shocking brilliant light. The one who carved into my leg rocked on the ground, hands cradling his head, trickles of red liquid falling through the cracks between his fingers.

My blade clattered on the concrete. Wobbling, I tried to grab the dagger with my right hand, but my depth perception had reset. My ears rang. I met concrete first, my left arm hanging limp against my body. I reached out again, catching my nails against concrete once more, peeling them backwards. Frustration and pain coated my groan. One more time. Finally, my shaking hand grasped the hilt.

I found the prisoner, curiously wearing a light grey jumpsuit, and stabbed at his neck until he stopped breathing. It was messy and it took far too much energy, but he was dead, haloed by his blood.

Only the fourth man still breathed. I grabbed at the bottom of my leather mask and peeled it off. I needed more vision, more accuracy. The leather fought against the movement, my sweat a glue that bound it to my skin. It tingled raw and red. Once the mask lay lifeless on the floor my vision began returning. I spat out the cotton ball, breathing in the scent of strong, harsh magic, like a fired cannon. It hit me like a god-gifted wave, all force and power. I growled.

The fourth prisoner had backed up and retreated several feet to the clay wall. His hands pressed against the unwilling structure. How had he moved so fast? My left arm still hung limp next to me as I staggered towards him. His eyes hadn't survived the bottled starlight, dripping in shades of brown, white and black liquid down his cheek.

"Kill me." His voice oozed metallic.

I made his death quick and merciful. The guilt threatened a sob in my throat, but I pushed through. These men could have been violent. The fourth man wore a respectable shade of orange, but they too were victims of the raging red magic that owned this level.

I felt it. It didn't stain the air a red hue like level six's brown magic. Invisible.

And yet, rage built inside me.

It energised me as a violent song tuning my thundering heart, though I knew not to trust it. My body should be weak. Yet every emotion, every fragment of feeling that wandered in and out of my mind, was completely and utterly intensified. I felt unstoppable. The rage I oozed toward the dead man who dislocated my shoulder was exaggerated. I knew this magic, I wore it on my belt. I looked down at my leg, peeling fabric from skin, a perfect circle carved from the man with a bleeding face. It stung more than a bite from a sea-bee.

My anxiety thrummed. Heart raced. Ant, I needed to save Ant. I was going to die. I would not save him. I had to. I would. I would tear this place apart. Everyone was as good as dead. I was as good as dead.

This would not do. My thoughts jumbled like a tangled rope.

The magic trinket had mercifully staved off the other nearby prisoners, who were either too injured, blinded or too overwhelmed by emotions to fight. They blinked away the remnants of the bright light.

I needed to calm myself. Breathe, I had time to breathe and think. My hand trembled on my thigh. With a curved spine, slowing my racing heart, I tried to remember the story of that one raised scar atop my thigh. My fingers traced it.

220 DAYS UNTIL CAPTURE:

Ant and I returned to our ship instead of seeking a healer on land. For a healer on land would talk, and I didn't want gossip.

I had forsaken independent movement and let Ant help me forward. His arm rested around my back. He was strong, but his height and size were comically difficult to navigate. He hunched to keep my arm around his shoulders. Eventually, when we made it onto the boardwalk, the mostly rotten wood that threatened a sprained ankle, Ant huffed and forced me into his arms, cradling me against my wishes.

"This is embarrassing," I mumbled.

I didn't make it easy for him to carry me. Instead of placing my arms around his neck like he asked, they sat across my chest. I was heavy for my size, covered in muscles, broad with a lifetime of training and fighting, and I

56

succumbed to that weight now, not that Ant acknowledged it. If he meant to treat me like a baby, I would act like one.

Ant was careful not to disrupt the knife protruding from my thigh. He almost tripped on a rotten hole in the last plank before climbing the few makeshift stairs that led us onto our deck. The air thinned with the salt of the ocean, tingling at my open wound but soothing my very soul.

"Oh, no!" Daphne laughed at the sight of me. "There goes your streak!"

It had been two years and eight months since my last stab wound. When I began my pirating calling, stabbings seemed far too common. I didn't have a knack for bartering, or a way of tact. My first three wounds had occurred within the first month of leaving my village. Odd how the language of magic-dealing pirates was written in the swings of a sword. It had killed that naive village girl, a hazing for my new life.

"Go get Will." Ant didn't look at Daphne as he barked orders, his gaze flickering between my wound and my scowl.

Daphne nodded, face set sternly, and hastened, a figure glittering gold. My vision faded, blood, pain and embarrassment lulling me into sleep. My pride had kept me conscious, but not for much longer.

"Stay awake, my cyclone." Ant gently placed me on the rug in our quarters moments before Willem opened the door.

Willem had been one of Ant's men. He was my favourite, perhaps because he couldn't speak after an assassination attempt left his larynx badly bruised. Will had gained employment as an Ovator's healer on the continent. The Ovator lived in excessive wealth and treated his staff with excessive unfairness too, like pets.

During a coup, the Ovator died. Will almost did too. Serendipitously, Ant had planned to rob the Ovator's estate that night.

I speculated if Ant killed the Ovator — he always claimed not to.

Ovators weren't supposed to deal in magic, but many did. And rumour held that this Ovator had a rather impressive collection. Ant saved Will and carried the lanky healer in his arms, out of the mansion and onto his ship. He was so impossibly thin, so underfed. Ant didn't steal magic trinkets that night, but perhaps something far more valuable.

Willem examined the knife sticking out of my thigh, pushing thick towels around my leg. He looked at me wordlessly, tucking a loose strand of wispy hair behind his ear, and began drawing the blade out, careful to mimic the exact path of entry. The knife worked like a plug as the blood pooled, caught by the clean towels. Thank the mother Navira had done laundry, or else we risked infection.

Ant gripped my hand as Will poured an open bottle of white liquor onto my wound. I screamed as he sterilised the end of a needle, then took a line of silk thread and began weaving it through my flesh.

My eye glistened with wrath as it investigated Ant's soft ones. His didn't leave my face.

"I would have killed her for you, Farrah, if you really wanted it," Ant said softly. "I would kill anyone for you."

And though the pain overwhelmed me, I believed him.

I recalled this pain as I grabbed my dangling arm, held it steady, lined it up and manipulated it back into its socket. The limb popped loudly. A wave of relief greeted the pain, the injury reducing from a gnawing to a hum. It would do. Although it would come out again, hopefully it'd last a few more levels.

Emotions disobeyed me. I grabbed at the now useless trinket on the concrete, the fuzzy trinket, no longer illuminated with dangerous promise, and held it up towards the Central Guard Tower, seething with fury.

"This was meant for you." Saliva dripped down to the floor as
I spat out, hurling the ball at my reflection
Yet they didn't react. My reflection mocked me.
They watched. They always watched.

My pants rested uncomfortably against my now-bleeding leg. The perfect circle pulsed on my skin, blood hardening around the fresh, permanent scar. Perhaps if I expected to survive the day, this would bother me. But the throbbing reminded me not to trust my emotions, not here.

I thought this, even as the words left me without direction.
"Who's next?

A prisoner scurried away.

My hand gripped firmly around my dagger once more. Steadying my breath, hoping logic would return, I considered picking up the plague mask and placing it back between my breasts and bindings, but something made me reconsider. Something told me it had done its job. I hoped that little voice was trustworthy. With the magic in the air, I had no ability to truly question it.

Prisoners recovering from the unexpected flash filled the small curve of the visible level. Good, the magic trinket did its job, but when I would turn the next bend, however – the places my magic didn't reach – the threats would continue.

But my next turn halted me.

The purpose of the Panopticon's design was that the Ovator Guards always watched. They had complete and utter sight. And yet, here, what lay before me was a maze, not made by the Panopticon or the Ovator Guards, but by prisoners. It was flimsy, cots were disassembled, rods stacked together to create makeshift walls barely six feet, thin cotton sheets obstructing all vision.

Curious. Disconcerting.

And the only way forward.

I favoured my better arm, grasping the dagger as I pushed forward. A tattered white cloth with a bloody circle signified the entrance to the maze. I pulled it to the side and shoved inside.

Without the orange hue of the clay walls, the maze glowed starkly bright. I blinked, sensitive. The shift in tone confused the path from eye to mind. Perplexed by the maze, I obeyed each turn. I could break through, push past the cotton walls, but something convinced me not to. Follow the maze, my mind told me, respect its path.

I made it past a frustrating dead end, turned back, and found the way forward. The maze was rudimentary, but my rage-fuelled mind struggled to best it.

Finally, I realised why this maze existed, why level four was the great equaliser.

The magic didn't hum red here for the prisoners. No, the magic was the consequence.

The first beast.

Beasts were stupid abominations. Not to be underestimated, since they were strong and vicious. They were also easily confused. Beasts could spend eternity without movement if nothing wandered into their vision. Drawn to the sight of prey, if they perceived movement, they'd pounce. They had no soul, no heart, existing just for god entertainment, a vessel of lifeless destruction.

I still recovered from the stab wound Ant's ex gifted me when Navira encountered her first beast.

199 DAYS UNTIL CAPTURE:

The gods no longer touched this land.

Neither Navira nor I had ever seen snow before. It was so rare. It sat softly on the tip of my tongue. The icy white flakes melted, leaving a prickle of sensitive frigidity. Soft, endless whiteness, the perfect coolness, a façade that hid the harsh, barren truth of the surrounding land.

Ant had been obsessive in his quest for the God Killer. We were so close. Just one more clue, the second-last puzzle piece. Ant, Navira and I walked forward.

Navira was no longer a child. She may never have truly been one. She'd been with us for years now, having chosen to stay. But as she stood there with hands outstretched and twirled as the snow fell faster, my heart clenched with adoration. I worried the snow would challenge her mind's white cage. She had been through so much. We all had — all three of us. I hoped this moment together, victorious as a family, would replace the nightmares.

Despite the flurry, the sky was a curious, clear shade of blue. It decorated the sky brightly. Warm enough that the sun's rays fought the cold, pillowy snow, and the sight energised us despite the long journey. Stillness coated the air.

Ant stiffened next to me. There, just ahead, the Cave. White curves carved into the cliff side, so pale against the blue sky, it barely materialised until we were steps away. Only the hint of shadows gave away its presence.

We had made it. The snow-covered mountains led us directly to the structure carved by man and beast.

Ant took the lead, and I followed, keeping Navira at my rear. The petite magic orb rested in one of his hands, knife in the other. I clasped my sword. Whilst the orb illuminated the cave walls, my sword shone with the lava of the very volcano that forged it.

The beast may have been dormant for decades. We didn't know. It surely guarded the contents of the cave, abandoned by a lazy, sightless god. The gleaming white skeletons that rested by its large, matted paws gave us hope that what we sought remained.

This beast was enormous — the biggest I'd ever seen. It towered over Ant, closest in form to a wolf but with features too mortal to be animal. With a pointed nose, thick fleshy lips, irises cuddled by pure white. Covered in a harsh brown fur, as though a god didn't know how to create a creature that didn't resemble its subjects. It smelled strongly of wet fur. It shook off layered ice that fell to the ground in fragments before charging towards Ant.

Ant and I had fought together for years now. We were completely in sync, a dance between us. This beast was no challenge. The orb sat on the floor, illuminating the narrow, frigid space. Our bodies shadowed it, but my blade shone bright. I breathed out, releasing a trickle of condensation.

Navira watched. She'd been training, perhaps ready for this fight, but even she knew not to interrupt our dance.

Navira didn't move as we dismembered the beast's limbs as the logical first move. The beast couldn't feel pain, so when it lost a leg, it struggled but didn't adapt. Its blood ran brown. Then, Ant's blade sawed through the neck until its head dangled, before tumbling to the ground with a thud. The only way to kill a beast — behead it.

I was grateful Navira wasn't here to make good on Ant's promise, even though I was certain she'd want to be.

Metal was poisonous to beasts. That was why blades were so effective. Vengeful gods made beasts to punish mortals, but didn't consider technology. Stupid, really. No one claimed gods were smart, just powerful. Without the gods, the mother could rule.

In the Panopticon, the prisoners had no metal. Maybe the legs of the cots, but they were too blunt to pierce through fur and flesh. This beast wasn't a threat to a skilled pirate or magic-dealer, but to the prisoners, it was a thing of nightmares. The maze their only defence. Ingenious, particularly on a level overwhelmed by chaotic magic. Without this maze, the beast would massacre every prisoner or force them downwards.

There was no escaping the Panopticon – only a quicker death.

It took both Ant and me to kill that one beast, but that beast had been more than double the size of this one. This one was small. It still smelled the same, like wet fur, the memory colouring the stark white of the Panopticon with remnants of that icy, cool blue cave.

Stalking towards me, the beast growled low in its belly, breath thick and roasting. No need for magic. The dagger would do.

When the beast charged at me, pointed teeth bared, I slid on the concrete ground until pressed under its fur. My body barely fit. I could feel it growl, vibrations moving through its thick coat, protecting a thumping heart. Fur tickled my face. It tried to shift forward, confused. I slid with it, hamstrings burning with mimicked movement. Fur obscured me. The beast could smell a challenger but couldn't see one. We moved in sync.

There was no need to waste energy on the limbs. I shimmied my body upwards until I settled below its neck and pressed my blade to its throat.

A beast was much easier to behead than a mortal. The metal blade burned through flesh as it gushed brown blood that rained down on me. Maybe it was the beasts' weakness. Maybe it was the imitation strength this level's magic gave me. The action teased with ease. The head thudded to the ground, dead eyes opened wide in dismay, as though they had never carried life. Maybe they really hadn't. Maybe it was a god trick. I contemplated leaving the head where it rested but reconsidered.

This was stupid, but I was all rage and emotion, propelled by blood lust. My blade clutched in my good hand, and my shoulder protested at the heaviness of the beast's head in my other. I held it by a tuft of fur, almost dragging it on the floor, unable to lift my arm higher. Brown blood pooled onto the concrete as I retraced my steps to the maze's entrance. My movements were sloppy, forgetting the way forward, slipping on the blood trail I was leaving, repeating the same steps.

Once I reached the torn cloth signifying the start of the maze, I pushed the beast's head out first, my shoulder protesting at its weight, then my body. At first, I held it up at the prisoners. Dozens watched with leaking uncertainty. Some still recovering from the flash rubbed their reddened eyes. Some just looked at me with veneration. A dry sea of grey and orange jumpsuits stared at me.

A destroyer. Destroyer of man and beast. What will she destroy next?

Then, I turned. I glowered at the Central Guard Tower.

My image stared back through the dark grey reflective surface. I looked manic. A small pool of beast blood sat in my empty eye socket. Wounds, blood and sweat peppered my skin. My curly raven hair matted with heavy moisture, no longer tamed by its braid. My chest heaved with exertion. I held the beast's head up to the Central Guard Tower and threw it with all my force, a force gifted from the level's magic.

It bounced off the mirror.

They watched. They always watched.

It took me far too long to retrace my brown-blood steps through the cotton maze, but no more beasts greeted me, and no prisoner dared follow. The sheets grew more blood-splattered towards the maze's exit, something fresh signifying a bloody story. There were no bodies though, just the signs of a struggle. A cocktail of wet and dried blood. Red and brown. The slaves who created the maze, killed by the thing they sought to contain.

Eventually, the thinnest cotton sheet imaginable – so thin that the colour of the clay walls shone through – opened to the exit. The darkness warmed my vision. I welcomed the shift in tone. Orange.

The hole down invited me. I had survived the middle level, beast, magic and all. One less magic trinket, covered in fresh scars. My thoughts swirled intrusive and unwanted, with hands shaking with rage. I fished out another glowing gold ball from my pouch, desperate to regain control and trust in my mind again.

I wanted to destroy and cry and kill and mourn, and I needed to focus.

The ball fell as I stood above the hole to the next level down. No smoke, no hue of magic.

Level three.

I had made it. I was more than halfway.

6. Level Three

The jump down became intuitive. I landed on the balls of my feet with knees pressing forward. As soon as I landed, the thirst, the hunger, the pain rolled back through me in waves that no longer propelled me forward but paralysed me. The ache no longer fuelled me. I sucked in a serrated breath.

The previous level was a lie. Was the beast real? The magic certainly was. I couldn't trust my emotions, but could I trust my memories?

My eye blinked. The first prisoner I saw cowered, literally cowered at me, and in his hand rested a wet cotton ball.

I pounced on him in an instant, blade against his throat. I snatched the cotton ball and flung it into my mouth before backing away once more. Then, I sheathed my blade. He didn't challenge me, instead, he retreated. And yet his jumpsuit was orange. A pale orange, dimmed with grey – but still.

The cotton ball felt drier than the one on level five, but I still managed a small gulp. It teased. Thirst took its toll, my muscles clenched across my body in fatigue, and my leg fought between a hamstring spasm and the uncomfortable ache of my ankle's freshly carved circle.

Level three's atmosphere thickened with the abundance of prisoners. Perhaps, the busiest level. They looked, but no one approached. They scurried through the same curved grey structure, cocooned by orange clay walls. Like they had jobs to do, their own personal missions to complete. I shifted my weight from one leg to the other. This level felt almost normal in a place far from it. I almost missed the ravenous, magic-crazed prisoners of the previous level. At least they made sense.

I peered at the Central Guard Tower as if it held the answers, but nothing. The identical, obscured circular Guard Tower still sat in the centre of the cell.

They watched. They always watched.

"Hello." A voice shook me out of my trance.

Exhaustion distracted me. Red magic left my body tired and depleted. I shook my head.

"Hello," I replied.

I examined the prisoner. His jumpsuit was the most curious thing – so utterly distracting. A patchwork of orange and grey, somehow stitched together. I narrowed my eye. The patches appeared sewn together with mortal hair, the thread a medley of shades and thickness. He wore it proudly, his chest puffed, donning a handmade cotton hat on his head, a cotton so dirty it appeared a yellowing beige.

"I am the king of this level." He spoke as if it were the most obvious thing in this world. "What business do you have here?"

I looked around again, really taking it in. The prisoners moved meekly under control. Each prisoner had one patch of jumpsuit missing, taken from their sleeve or their pant leg, but always visibly missing. They looked at me with curiosity but didn't linger, as though lingering came at a cost. They just moved with purpose, with structure. "King?"

I should not be curious.

The prisoner nodded. "Yes, as I just said. I am king. What business do you have here?"

I bit my bottom lip, analysing how to proceed. He was the first prisoner who dared converse, dared speak first. And he hadn't tried to kill me – at least, not yet.

"I wish for safe passage to the next level down."

The Prisoner King seemed as inquisitive of me as I of him, though his brown eyes held a peculiar emptiness. His thin lips looked like he only smiled in ire, not joy.

He raised a hand, a hand red and raw, to his chin and pondered. "Level two is no place for a fair lass." He shifted a little. "What's that in your eye?"

I grumbled, sick of my goddamn eye being such a spectacle. Maybe disposing of that lens was a mistake. "It's just blue. Surely, you've seen blue eyes."

He ruminated as though he sought to reclaim a memory long forgotten. "It isn't just a colour. You're the ocean before a storm."

These men and their goddamn oceans. I tried not to let my annoyance show, for I should tread carefully. Maybe if I had spent weeks in an ocean-less desert prison, I would crave it too. I considered smacking my hand on my head, but it still dripped with the remnants of beast blood. Mixed with the blood of several prisoners, of course.

As if following my vision, the Prisoner King said, "I can give you safe passage through, my lass, and a swab to clean that blood, and I only ask for one thing in return."

I almost didn't want to know. He pointed at me.

"That golden thing. I want it."

My golden monocular. I thought back to that icy cave, how long it had taken for us to find it. Could I really gift it to a Panopticon prisoner, after all we sacrificed?

Navira worried about the beast's corpse as we wandered further down the path of the cave, as though it might reanimate and bite her. The temperature dropped, even without the falling snow, the air undisturbed for years. At the very centre, carved into icy stone, sat the golden monocular, a seer's greatest accomplishment. The gold was at odds with the blue ice it sat upon. It was the only known remaining monocular. The Ovators sought to destroy magic trinkets, and this was one of the most dangerous to their gods.

Ant picked it up but didn't dare use it, not yet. He respected magic deeply. We wordlessly followed him out of the cave and began the long journey back to our ship. By the time we returned, the ship sat in inch-deep frozen water. It would be a pain to free.

Only once on deck did I let my heavy breath escape. We had done it. Ant placed the monocular in a box in our quarters, the three of us staring down at its beauty. None of our crew bothered us.

"It's beautiful," I said, watching the gold coating shimmer.

The golden monocular hummed with magic. It should, for it was the most powerful tool to detect magic. It was even prophesied to see the exact location of the God Killer, even at the bottom of the deepest, darkest, most dangerous ocean. This was our most perilous step. And we had done it.

"It sure is."

But it was me Ant stared at as he picked me up and twirled me with infectious glee. He almost giggled. My legs lifted as he spun faster, kissing my cheeks, my neck and my lips.

Navira rolled her eyes at the affection, though I could tell she was excited about the magic, too. Her sparkling hazel eyes sang the tune. She shook her head and walked towards the door.

"How long until we leave?" She stole one more longing look at the magic trinket.

"Soon." Ant still didn't look away from me.

"Why?" I asked, sparing only a glance her way.

"I need to take my medicine."

"Still?"

This admission got Ant's attention, and Navira looked away from his unfiltered stare with a blush. The first time she admitted she got seasick, we almost threw her back on land to deal with the ashen corpses of her former home. But Willem carried those pills. Those black round pills. They quenched the waving waters, the threatening vomit, soothed her stomach. Now, before every adventure, she took one. She always said she was no pirate, but a peasant in disguise.

Ant regretted his question and spared her an apologetic glance. "Soon, little pirate. First, I must make love to my captain."

With that, Navira grumbled, slamming the door to our quarters behind her. Ant and I shared a laugh.

I couldn't be sentimental about it, not now. It had fulfilled its purpose. It led me down here. My hand fought my mind as I unclipped the monocular and handed it to the Prisoner King. It looked hideous on his blotchy skin.

He brought it to his eye, but I stopped him.

"Wait!" I said, a hand touching his red raw skin as I closed the gap between us. "That is sharp and dangerous magic. If you wish to lose an eye, go ahead."

He considered me, my missing eye, lowering the monocular before he said, "Thank you, lass. Now, let's get you cleaned up."

He placed the monocular in the top pocket of his jumpsuit, where the darkest orange fabric sat, the gold peeking above his breast.

"How long have you been king here?" I asked as he ushered me forward, his hands clasped behind his back.

Being next to the king seemed to give me some sort of immunity. No one dared to even stand close. They respected him –

somehow – in this lawless place. Respected or feared. What did the Ovator Guards make of this?

"For a minute, for a month, for a millennium." The king's voice was far too casual for the weight of his words.

Time. Time did not move here like outside. The stagnation. He didn't know.

"Was there a king before you?" "Yes." He pointed at his cotton hat.

No.

Not cotton, flesh. I swallowed bile. His hat wasn't made from the dull cotton of the cots, but instead, dried skin. Mortal leather, still covered in thin, fine hair. The Panopticon humbled me once more, and I suppressed questions for fear of awakening the rage of the Prisoner King. My heart raced.

"Ahh!" The Prisoner King clapped as we arrived at a small makeshift bench.

A cot had been stretched so that the fabric was taut, and on top sat a few folded pieces of fabric. Next to them, a curious glass jar. The liquid inside it was clear, but as soon as the king picked up the jar and opened the lid, the undeniable scent of alcohol pickled my nose. My stomach grumbled, throat bobbing in disappointment.

The king either didn't notice my thirst and hunger, or he ignored it. He grabbed a piece of fabric and liberally coated it with the alcohol before pressing it in my hand.

"There," he said.

I looked down at the rag for a split second before muttering a thanks and wiping my hands. They stung. Minor cuts sprinkled across them, either from the nails of prisoners on former levels or from my blade. I didn't know why and didn't care. I wiped the red and brown splotches before dabbing my neck and my face. It hurt – prompting memories of the boils in the sun, then that first prisoner who scratched me. How long ago was that now? Time stagnated. It could be hours. It could be days.

Soon, that small piece of fabric wore more blood than my skin, and I was grateful for it. Felt lighter for it, too.

The small moan wasn't meant to leave my mouth, and I regretted it in an instant. The king's pupils dilated before he regained composure. I wanted to ask another question, to ask how they got the alcohol, where the bottle came from. Yet my curiosity went unquenched. The fleshy hat he wore bore his insanity much more than the false lucidity on his face. There was nothing more dangerous than a deranged man with a brain.

"Thank you." I tried to sound genuine and casual but failed at one of those.

"Your skin is far too pretty to be covered in blood, my lass." Was the king flirting with me?

I scoffed, pretending to adjust my belt, making sure the dagger still sat against my hip. The king didn't notice this move. He appeared transfixed – completely and utterly transfixed – on my eye.

Perhaps this should have been the first ominous sign, but it was when we continued through the level, past the bustling prisoners, that I noticed more makeshift tables. These too had little jars filled with alcohol, but the jars weren't empty.

Fucking hell.

Eyes.

Eyeballs filled the jars. Each cot lined the wall, fabric taut, with at least three to five jars placed like trophies atop. Each jar held one to two eyes, as though they stared back at the Central Guard Tower. Mostly matching sets but, curiously, a few contained different colours.

I was wrong to assume that this man had not seen blue eyes. He collected them.

The jars didn't just display blue. One even had a pair of green eyes. Green eyes had long been assumed extinct, but here they were, sitting in an alcohol solution, preserved in time. Some jars held eyes that were beautiful shades of hazel and brown.

One caught me between steps, and I faltered. No, it couldn't be. I would know that shade of golden brown. Last time I saw it, it kicked me off our ship. Just one eye, just one eye preserved in time.

"Where did you get that eye?" I unsheathed my dagger and pointed it toward the king's throat.

He winced and stepped back, so consumed by my eye that he hadn't realised I investigated the jars. A flash of something deep sat across the king's face. Mortification or shame, maybe.

"That was a gift," he quaked.

The other prisoners stared as I rested the glistening, mahoganytipped blade against the Prisoner King's bobbing throat. Would they fight me? Were they willing to die for their king? I didn't care. I didn't care about anything, about dying, fighting. That was my lover's eye in that jar. My soulmate.

I knew we wouldn't live past the Panopticon, but my heart still broke for him. He had always tried to understand how my limited vision impeded my life. Now he lived it, and he did so alone.

The enucleated eye made me doubt if Ant still lived, though the evidence proved that he'd made it down to the third level. It should give me hope, but it did the opposite. My other hand patted the small velvet bag of medicine on my belt, thumbing around until I skimmed those two perfectly round black pills. He wouldn't leave this world, not without me.

Between forcing Navira off the ship and setting sail for the God Killer, we stumbled across the death dealer when seeking an Enchantress.

29 DAYS UNTIL CAPTURE:

"She will never forgive us," I sighed.

We left Navira at the nearby nameless town. She made a friend or two there, as we passed through frequently, and had lodging and money. She liked the tavern owner, even though he hated me. My guilt gnawed.

Ant's body bumped against mine as we meandered along the isle's boardwalk, until we traversed through wet dirt, further away from the safety of our crew. Night prevailed, though in this dreadful place, I didn't know if day even existed. The isle edged against the Rain Isles but was the only piece of land overseen by the Swamp God. Large mangroves blocked our line to the stars, and even if they didn't, the clouds were so thick they consumed the sky. Tiny eyes peered down at us from above. I shivered.

Ant said nothing as his warm hand grasped mine, his big fingers woven through my petite ones. He fed me with strength the miserable and peculiar surroundings depleted from me.

Only one woman resided in the depths of this swampy wasteland. She was the woman we sought. An Enchantress.

The rumour was that the Enchantress and Swamp God were lovers, that she broke his heart, and he banished her to immortality amongst the mortals and ghouls. No one knew for certain, but she was granted refuge in this swampland, despite dealing in the most dangerous forms of magic.

Dark magic.

Trinkets collated magic without purpose, but some were so deadly and dangerous even Ovators refused to wield them. The trinkets here couldn't be created by seers, the magic too forbidden. Not seer magic, not god magic, certainly not mother magic — something unknown.

Perhaps she used to be a seer, but now was something without a name.

"She will." Ant looked down at me, too long between words. "Once we've gotten the God Killer and— "

Ant faltered. Before us, when the mangroves parted, stood a wooden dwelling. The wood wore a rich mahogany stain, but the iron gate surrounding it stopped us. Skulls in various stages of decomposition hung from iron railheads. Some were completely sun-bleached bone, others so fresh, the muscle and skin of identities looked lifelessly down at us as if in warning.

Leave, they whispered.

"Home sweet home." Ant smirked lopsidedly.

"We can use it as inspiration for our ship decorating," I joked, tightening my grip on his hand.

"If things go wrong," I said, "not that I'm worried or anything, but if things go wrong, promise you'll look after her."

He sent me a sideways look. "She's family, she'll always be safe, she'll always be loved. Plus, we aren't in real danger. It's a house. What do you think will happen?

I grumbled. "It's a house decorated with skulls."

"Not our skulls."

"Not yet."

At this, Antorn smiled. "You've triumphed against mortal enemies, flesh dealers, Ovators, beasts and krakens. A little home in the woods is your undoing?" I straightened. He was right.

He dropped my hand, squeezed my hip and planted a soft kiss on my forehead. "Ready?" I nodded.

We came without weapons. The drunk pirate with the curious arm in the tavern stressed it was the most important rule when approaching the Enchantress. Stressed through slurs. The gates swung open for us with an eerie creak. We walked up the makeshift path outlined with a putrid bog.

Ant knocked twice on the dwelling's front door using a goldplated handle. Carved in the shape of the beast, the metal dulled as a cheap imitation, like its maker hadn't ever seen one, but sought to exude fear. It thudded and moaned at the intrusion.

The Enchantress was nowhere as the front door swayed open. The room contracted with shadows and showed only a small fraction of what it held. Charcoal walls, a carpeted violet floor, and emptiness. A peculiar, delicate scent of rotten patchouli and wood. And there, on a pillar facing the front door, sat the thing we sought.

"How did she know?" I whispered, but Ant shushed me.

The fishing rod was unlike anything I had ever seen. Blue, its wire shifting between all the shades of the open ocean. Ant placed down the bag he gripped, the bag of offerings to even this trade. Rare magic trinkets, gold and silver. It was worth nothing to us now that we had the Trench Rod. He picked it up, but it was I who faltered.

"The man who owns this eye would never gift it to you."

My blade sat so tightly against the Prisoner King's throat that a bead of blood dripped downwards. I didn't understand how this man could overpower someone like Ant. I wasn't short myself, but Ant towered over me, and I stood a similar height to the Prisoner King. Yet the proof existed in the jar.

The king's eyes widened with fear, puzzlement, excitement and lust. I didn't like the combination. Though the Central Guard Tower sat at my back, I knew they watched.

They always watched.

Would killing their Prisoner King be what finally won their company?

When he didn't answer, I tried another approach. "How long ago was he here?"

"A minute, a month, a m—"

I cut him off. "Give me a real answer."

My spit landed on his cheek. He winced, paused, then met it with one long swipe of his tongue. He pondered, brows furrowed, his body twitching as it fought through the haze of the Panopticon, before he stared at the glass jar which housed Ant's eye. It was his left one, I realised, the tiny little specks of yellow signifying it.

"The jar," he said, pointing. "See how the top is dark grey, almost brown?"

I looked at the jar. He was right. Dark liquid marred the colour of the alcohol, dingy browns and greys. Not only that, but an inky pool floated at its very top.

"The colour. It means the eye has been in there for maybe a few days at most. It isn't red, so not fresh, but it hasn't lightened, so less than a few weeks. Lass, please, I swear it was a gift—"

I wanted to slit his throat. Of everyone, he deserved it the most. I didn't care that the prisoners on the former levels attacked me. I understood it. They were desperate, hungry, plagued, dying. This man, though, this man who collected the eyes of others, who wore the skin of his former king, the fabric of those he ruled, deserved it.

But maybe he deserved to live more than he deserved to die. Maybe someone finally deserved what waited for them on level one.

I grabbed Ant's eye jar and clutched it to my chest. "Take me to the entrance to level two now."

The Prisoner King made to protest, his gaze darting from my blue eye to Ant's golden brown one as though I stole his favourite toy. Eventually, he conceded.

"Fine, lass," he muttered.

My dagger sat on his spine as he led me forward, away from the nosy prisoners and towards the entrance down. Occasionally, we didn't just pass eye jars on benches, but jars held in prisoner hands, the prisoner acting as a statue. The first prisoner rested his back against the clay, his hand trembling as he gripped a tepid jar filled with a blue and hazel eye.

He whispered, "Cold, so cold."

A punishment, maybe. I didn't look around until seeing the next hole.

Once more, the space vacant, the hum of the way down frightened off nearby bodies. No trophies rested this close to the entrance down.

The grey pipe lingered on the wall. It had the same spout at the top, the same opening out of reach.

"What is that?" I pointed my blade upwards.

"The gift from the gods." The Prisoner King salivated. "When we are blessed, it will pour."

"So, that's where your water comes from?"

The Prisoner King turned towards me. My dagger sat on his chest as he leaned forward, the edge of the blade pressing against a seam in his jumpsuit.

"Not water. Power."

The king's hands wrapped around the hilt before I could even react. I was too distracted, fixated on the pipe. So fucking stupid. He was strong, well fed, well nourished. Probably taking the rations of those around him. I wasn't, still sobering from the red magic. We tumbled to the ground, my waning strength evidenced by my failing limbs, as he pried the dagger out of my hands and stood.

His eyes were wide circles, fixed on my one. He snarled, with sharpened teeth.

"I will put your eye with his, I promise," he said, looking between my eye and the jar. "Little lass, I have been waiting for an eye like yours for a minute, for a month, for a millennium." No, my heart thudded. No, I couldn't lose an eye, not again.

He gripped my dagger in one hand, the other pressed me to the ground, settling on top of my chest. I considered the remaining trinkets on my belt, but there was nothing that could be done here, unless I swallowed a black pill. But not yet. I couldn't see the entrance to the level down, not from where I lay. Could I make it? I had to try.

I pushed upwards, jumping to my feet in one last thrust of power, driving the king backwards, seeing the hole in the distance grow bigger. No time for the magic golden ball, not now. My hands gripped the very outside of the circular opening, but a convincing grip seized me and pulled. There was nothing to grab, just slick grey concrete. The tap of my fingers orchestrated a solemn tune.

He flipped me over, placing one knee over my chest. I tried to gasp, to wheeze. The sheer force of his body weight on mine was paralysing. He stared over me, dagger held between his fingers, tracing the circle of my eye in the air. I tried to punch him, but his other knee came down on my arm. I raised my other one, dropping Ant's eye, but it still ached with the dislocation. My punches on the back of his shoulder were ineffective, so much so that he barked a laugh in return.

"This will but take a moment, lass," the Prisoner King growled.

And that was it. That gold glimmer within his breast pocket. My free hand worked without thought. I shimmed it between our bodies and grabbed for the monocular. Gold and leather smoothed the outside, but as I reached around it, my finger prickled against the jagged crystal lens. The magic ran through the minor wound. I didn't think, didn't stop, just forced the monocular upwards, lens first, and into the eye of the Prisoner King.

His wail vibrated off the circular walls in echoes, a cry of a loss greater than death. He didn't drop the dagger as his hands lifted to his bleeding eye. The monocular struck true. Right in the centre of his iris.

Shards didn't pierce an eye like flesh, but they squished and slurped as the eye collapsed, sagging uselessly beneath the metal.

His weight faltered enough for me to crawl backwards. He fell to his knees, unfettered mania watching me with spilling blood. I didn't wait for him to recover, for he still had my blade, and it was only a matter of time before his fury met his strength. I bolted, grabbing Ant's eye and locating the opening to the entrance down. And jumped through.

The Prisoner King would fight me no more.

No time for magic, no time for tests, no longer armed.

Level two.

7. Level Two

"Oh, hi there."

I groaned. Again? I descended with far less grace than on the previous levels. My shoulder dislocated as I rolled downwards, as evidenced by a loud pop. In my haste to leave, I hadn't minimised my fall, prioritising the glass jar in my hand. Ant's eye. Safe.

"Please don't tell me you're the king of level two." I stood as I inserted my shoulder back in place, gripping Ant's eye between my thighs. It didn't go in as smoothly this time, stale throbs its reward.

He wasn't. At least this prisoner, wearing a light grey jumpsuit, obscuring my vision to the level, didn't look like he commanded an entire floor. He stood where I landed, with a small piece of parchment in one hand and a writing device in the other. My presence had startled him. He kept peering up towards the ceiling, as if waiting for someone else to come down – a low hum vibrated from his throat. Hazel eyes darted from me to the Central Guard Tower in quick flicks.

"King." The prisoner frowned, with wrinkles etched into leathery skin. "No, there is no king here. I am the weapons master."

"I have no weapon," I said, the reality of my predicament weighing heavily on my mind.

Down here, down with the prisoners that had already survived five levels of famine, magic, plague and power, there would be greater threats. My dagger was now in the possession of an utterly abhorrent man. The Prisoner King possessed a blade to take what wasn't his. But the consolation tugged at my lips – he lost an eye. No blade would bring that back. It wasn't even preserved in a jar. Mutilated by magic.

And I gained one eye. Ant's eye returned awkwardly to my hand, too big to place on my belt and too fragile to hold. Instead, and to the amusement of the weapons master, I shoved the jar down the front of my linen tunic, in bindings so that my breasts squished against the cool glass.

It would do, I supposed. Though it rested uncomfortably. Not like Ant hadn't seen it all before a thousand times over. I hoped it wouldn't cook.

"Of course you don't. What do I call you?"

The man studied his parchment with tremendous interest. I tried to peer over, curious what the scribbles could be, but he swiftly brought it to his chest with a huff.

"Name?" He shifted between his feet.

I didn't want to give my real name, and it was a curious gift for the Panopticon, where prisoners became a colour. Though only the gods had names with power, it wasn't the Panopticon's to own.

"Michel." Ant's last name.

Thinking about Ant, how far I'd come, yet how far we were from impossible freedom, tugged at the last of my sanity. I thought of that last time together, that last night.

We had done it. We found the location of the God Killer.

1 DAY UNTIL CAPTURE:

It lay in the deepest part of the Rain Isles. Thunder rumbled a deafening beat, rain pelting down like liquid darts. We leaned over the ship, using the golden trinket. The golden monocular pierced through every deluge of rain, even as large pink bursts of lightning illustrated the night sky.

There.

Without the monocular, we wouldn't know where to paddle the rowboat and cast the Trench Rod. But with it, the power moved through the layers of ocean and into Ant's wide grin. He handed me the monocular. I looked through, carefully hovering the crystal edge off my eye. If only Navira could see our triumph. Best she couldn't, best she was safe.

The sea remained darkened, illuminated not by light or colour, but by a haze of extraordinary motion. A halo of shifting atoms. I sniffed. Did it smell like burning plastic? Sharp, bitter, pungent. My nose twitched. As soon as I dropped the monocular, as soon as I looked away, the smell vanished.

I grinned too. Ant's elation was infectious.

"We fish, my cyclone." He stood behind me, the heat of his body sending a shiver down my spine. "We fish, and then we kill a god."

"Excuse me?" The man's voice intruded on my thoughts.

"Sorry, why did you need my name? And what did you ask?" I rubbed the ache in my shoulder as my eye snapped to the prisoner.

"To enter," he replied simply.

"Enter what?" I grew impatient.

"The contest for level one, you get to choose your weapon first." He frowned. "Surely you – never mind. So, what will it be, Michel?"

I balked. A contest? I scanned the surroundings and, sure enough, placed purposefully against the surrounding clay walls, where that grey pipe rested, was an abundance of rudimentary weaponry. Some metal, some crafted, but nothing as intricate and well balanced as my dagger. My dagger now in the hands of a deranged lunatic. A mace, club with glued barbs and several types of spiked gloves sat tempting but unworthy. The most curious piece of weaponry was a breastplate made of avisale skin, earthy colours glistening with a hint towards its mystical beauty. Nothing called to me. Until…

My heart lurched in my chest.

My sword.

It looked dull, as if it hid. The blade no longer shone brilliantly silver, hilt dimmed brown, not its usual red and gold hues, and its engravings were dormant. It camouflaged as an old and rusting stick, as if it would shatter with the whispering breeze. But I knew it was my sword. The sword I lost my eye for, the sword crafted from the lava of an erupting volcano, the only one in existence. In the corner of my eye, red fire burned deep within it.

How the hell did it end up here?

"That one." I pointed at my sword and tried to keep the tremble from my voice.

"Ahh, good choice," the man lied.

He didn't know.

The last time I saw my sword, it was on the ship with Ant. He kicked me off before the Ovators captured him. They must have brought it here to be used in the Panopticon. Our entire ship plundered, but the sword was too smart. It probably looked like a poorly made blade to them, something a moment away from breaking. Not enough to throw out, but certainly enough to steal. Perhaps all these weapons were looted from the prisoners within these walls.

The prisoner ushered me forward. The few steps it took for me to reach my sword stretched like an eternity. It hummed. My body struggled to still. As soon as my right hand grasped the hilt – the hilt engraved with markings signifying the twelve volcanoes, one active and eleven dormant – it glowed. It purred.

Even the weapons master flinched at the sight.

I was hungry and thirsty. I was bruised, bleeding and burnt. But now, I was complete. I felt full once more. Strong. Not the false strength of the red magic, but the strength that rested in a moveable home.

"Where is your overseer?"

The weapons master once more peered at the hole above us as if waiting for someone to drop. There would be no one, of course. Just darkness and shadows. I didn't take the usual route down.

"I don't have one." Enamoured by the warm hilt in my hand, I didn't bother looking at the weapons master.

"Well, everyone has one," he scoffed.

"Not me."

The man scribbled furiously on his parchment, wet ink dripping onto the concrete floor. His eyes darted towards the Central Guard Tower, as if waiting for confirmation. But none came.

They watched. They always watched.

"Looks like I'm good to go." I smirked at the Guard Tower and threw it the middle finger.

If the weapons master noticed, he said nothing.

"You have one hour to practice with your new weapon." The weapons master returned to the script he had memorised. "Then you will face three prisoners of your overseer's choice."

He looked at me then, chewing on his lip, uncertain how to proceed.

"So, my choice?" I raised an eyebrow.

I had no overseer.

He shrugged. This man may have the ink and the paper, but he had no power here. The light colour of his grey jumpsuit gave this away. It was a miracle he had made it this far. How long would it be until he was forced to fight, forced to die? Was there honour in working for the Ovator Guards, honour in watching his fellow prisoners fight?

"Rules are simple," he went on. "You may only use your weapon or your body."

He looked at my breasts, the glass jar pressed against my heart. Although I had no plan to use Ant's eye and glass jar as a weapon, I couldn't help but think of inventive ways of killing with it.

I could open the lid, grip the eyeball and—

"You cannot end the fight. You cannot concede. The fight only ends when one of you no longer breathes."

The weapons master waited for a reaction, but I just stared. Death was all this place promised. This level smelled like death, like heated iron and dread, but it had been a long time since that scent wrinkled my nostrils with disgust. Death and I were too familiar.

"Come with me," he said.

The further we walked, the more the level two battle space materialised. The Panopticon wasn't intuitively designed for a fight, with its singular curved space. Whatever this was, it appeared makeshift and impermanent. Perhaps the Ovator Guards on this level were bored, or they figured prisoners could be more than mere victims of torture. They could be the entertainment. To please gods with violence.

Towards the clay wall rested a line of sectioned-off practice zones. The grey partitions didn't work to obscure the vision of the Central Guard Tower. No, instead, they blocked the view of contestants from each other, leaving the space towards the centre open.

We moved past two contestants already in their individual practice zones. One wielded a large club and perspired dreadfully. Another sat slumped against the clay floor, blood pooling from his temple and hand, a small sob falling from his throat. The reaper's claw lingered at his throat.

I hoped he was my first contestant.

We stopped at the first free space. It was mostly empty, but there, on a glossy grey table, sat a small glass of water and a plate of brown gruel. It was the most beautiful, runny, disgustingly beige-looking plate of food I had ever laid my eye on. My mouth watered.

As if sensing my hunger, the weapons master clapped a hand on my back. "Eat, drink, regain your energy. Your hour starts now."

He left me alone within my personal space, tinged with the scent of blood and bleach.

My hands hovered over the plate of food, mouth watering so much I had to swallow. The glass's beautifully clear liquid danced in soft movement as I considered its vessel in trembling hands. A prize. But prizes down here weren't free. Prizes never were.

1 DAY UNTIL CAPTURE:

Ant and I took the ship's rowboat over to the exact position of the God Killer. Much to Daphne's dissent. There was no alternative. Even the rowboat would prove difficult to traverse through the rough waters and torrential downpour, but it was our best option.

We made the choice for two reasons. One, this was a fool's mission that Ant had already sacrificed so much for. There was a chance we would earn the wrath of at least one god, and our crew didn't need to wear the marks of that fury. Two, whilst our ship was much sturdier and provided some respite from the harsh winds and rain, the Trench Rod would be difficult to manage over the port side of such a big ship. The shimmering blue fishing rod we gained from the Enchantress manoeuvred easier from just above the waves.

We were soaking. I couldn't tell how much of my body dripped with the salty water of the waves or the harsh minerals of the rain. Either way, we were both drenched. We stared at each other as we paddled, one rough push through the thick water at a time.

Despite the utter gravity of our predicament, I couldn't help but admire Ant's beauty. His white shirt clung to the muscular curves of his body, and the wetness turned the material translucent. All his scars, all his stories, shone through like beautiful misery. Some scars we had experienced together. Some I may have caused. But that beautiful, perfectly imperfect body told a story that was the closest to a fairytale as anything I could have hoped for. And if this was how our story ended, at least we ended it together.

His long brown hair floated in a loose ponytail at his back. The moonlight flickered between dark clouds, catching the gold in his brown eyes. He looked so determined, so ready to face death, to be the first mortal to kill a god. I had never wanted more. "Farrah." He used my name. "You've stopped paddling."

I masked my expression and continued rowing, the waves concrete against my strokes. We had gotten far too scrawny on this task, rationing food and water for weeks. Too long between shore visits. My usually muscular arms had thinned, frail and weak, skin fastening to bone. Ant had amassed so much strength in his lifetime that it still clung desperately to his body. He did practically all the work, anyway.

"Where did you go?" he asked.

Although his voice struggled over the storm, it was the most beautiful thing I had ever heard, like a sound capable of penetrating the greatest roar.

The Trench Rod hummed to life. Beneath our boat rested a blackness deeper than any mortal eye could decipher. And beneath that lay the God Killer.

I never told him where my mind had gone, how looking at him felt like lightning hitting the very centre of my being, that when I woke, I moved for him, and that he had stolen not just my heart, but every cell that clung to my imperfect body.

Instead, we had work to do.

I may have never told Ant all the ways I loved him with words, but my actions would talk louder.

The table's content faltered me. I knew not to trust the food and water. They were products of the Panopticon, after all. I considered my trinkets. The different coloured medicine pills weren't helpful in this exact predicament. Instead, I picked out a golden ball from my canvas pouch and placed it between my fingers, hovering it above the water. Though used to detect magic through the air, the water would contain enough oxygen to work similarly. At least, that was the theory.

The golden ball splashed into the small glass. I hoped and prayed to the mother, swirling the cup in my hand. I waited. Nothing. Nothing happened. My hands shook as I took a shallow sip.

It took every ounce of willpower not to gulp down every drop of water. The glass was too small to quench my thirst completely. I paused, considered the taste, the smell, my body, then took another sip. My gaze then drifted to the plate of gruel. It smelled of nothing. The nothingness didn't reassure me – food should have a scent.

The food wouldn't contain enough oxygen to detect any magic with a golden ball. Plus, magic wasn't consistent. If the ball covered only a portion of the runny food, it could miss the trace of magic. I hungered, yes, but I had gone longer without food. I had only two levels left. The food sat tempting but untouched.

How many idiots before me had refused the food? I glanced at the Central Guard Tower.

They watched. They always watched.

There wasn't much to practice, careful not to waste too much energy. My body still ran warm from all the death and destruction it had wielded across the levels. Plus, the sword sat perfectly in my hand. Reunited. It was made for me. I sacrificed my eye for its power. I moved across the partitioned area, shifting my body and blade as one, blade slicing through the air with a crisp swish, like the first beat of a siren's call. My ultimate weapon. Not the monocular. Not a Trench Rod. Certainly not that cursed God Killer.

1 DAY UNTIL CAPTURE:

Ant took on the burden of wielding the Trench Rod. Despite releasing the rowboat's anchor into the sea, there was no bottom for it to grasp. And yet, we floated perfectly still, held by an invisible force.

The gods were possessive beings. Perhaps they fought against each other now, fought either to kill us or to let us succeed. Whatever it was, they wavered at an impasse. The rowboat barely swayed, waves slowing, rain halting to a gentle trickle.

It was strange seeing Ant fishing in the middle of the ocean in the dead of the night. He went to stand, but the boat tipped with his uneven weight. Instead, he knelt, throwing the fishing line over his shoulder, then into the ocean. I had never seen such a wellmade rod. Traditional rods were crafted of flimsy wood, but the Trench Rod had been carved of crystal and stone, irradiated with the moonlight. Every shade of blue imaginable. Even the line felt like silken diamond.

In the blink of my eye, Ant vanished from the rowboat. I sat alone, the gentle sound of rain no longer penetrating past the fear of loss. Panic erupted in my blood as I scanned the sea. I jumped up, almost slipping into the endless midnight. The stagnant waves provided the only movement. I steadied myself. The rowboat was small. He couldn't hide. He was no longer here. No longer with me.

"Ant!" I screamed, paralysed as I scanned the ocean. The ocean that seemed oppressively big, veiled by the onslaught of new rain that prickled my skin.

Our ship sat in the distance. The clouds shifted over the moon.

Waves swayed the rowboat gently. No Ant.

He had gone.

It felt like an aeon until he materialised back on the boat. No longer gripping the Trench Rod, but the largest, most omnipotent blade I had ever seen. I almost cowered. The hilt was midnight blue. Embossed symbols of the gods wrapped around it. Even the blade was carved with symbols that had lost their meaning. It didn't reflect the moonlight – it stole it purring. The God

Killer changed the very fabric of the surrounding air and brought back the deluge.

Ant's eyes met my blue one. His trembled with shadows.

We never discussed what had happened, where he went, or what he saw. The Ovators found us the next day.

"Michel!"

A different prisoner shook me from my thoughts. The collector – he called himself. I observed the collector with the light orange jumpsuit and considered the role he played in this game.

"Yes?" I gripped my sword.

"Your time is up."

He danced impatiently between his feet. I guessed that the Ovator Guards were happy for me to play. Swallowing regret, I considered the untouched food before sipping the last drops of water. Better to be hungry than potentially poisoned. I tipped the glass up so high that the back of my neck ached.

I made to leave but faltered, the glass jar still pressing against my chest. It was folly to keep Ant's eye on me, particularly when prisoners would aim for the heart. It could become a weapon, become embedded within my breastbone. Slick sweat stuck to the glass jar as I fumbled it on the table. Surely, I would return here if I won. Surely, I could get it back and return it to its owner.

The prisoner walked me past a few more partitioned training zones. Some were occupied, others with empty plates and glasses. Only one other prisoner didn't touch their food or water. Perhaps they died before they could.

We walked until we made it past the last partition and towards an opening. An orange chalked circle decorated the concrete floor, the shade matching the surrounding walls. This was where the fighting occurred, one battle at a time, an impermanent game, waiting to be destroyed.

The previous fight was yet to finish. Two prisoners battled, the omnipotent Guard Tower the only witness. Elusive watchers, always in control. Fresh and dry blood dyed the concrete in messy splotches. The whole place reeked of sweat. A prisoner in the darkest, deepest orange towered over another. I watched as the big, burly prisoner shoved a long, thin blade into his opposition's throat. His final blow, a cry of agony. My breath caught.

Ant.

8. Still Level Two

Ant was here. Not on level one, he was here.

He'd won his fight, his first or last? Based on the blood covering his flesh, the red that blended with the dark orange of his jumpsuit, probably not his first.

Initially, I didn't see the hole where his left eye once occupied. Long strands of dull brown hair hid it. For a split second, I wondered if I had grabbed someone else's eye, that a stranger's eye ogled my breasts as I carried it through the level. But no, Antorn pushed the sleeve of his jumpsuit upwards, his veins dark with dehydration, and wiped a strand of hair behind his ear. The eye was missing. A small part of me mourned with him. It was an undeniable tragedy when a permanent part of you no longer existed, something that couldn't grow back, that the body couldn't replicate.

Yet, even without the eye, he'd won. His opponent lay lifeless, engulfed in his own blood, eyes wide open in permanent, unwelcome death. Perhaps the weeks Ant trained with me, learning how to adapt to the challenges of changed vision, helped. But I also knew the truth. Time was my biggest advantage, and he had little left.

He looked unwell. Alive, yes, but without the former glory of whom I once knew. The orange jumpsuit contrasted pale grey skin, and whilst he stood tall and broad, the past several weeks had taken a toll on his health. Chasms of thin flesh and bone protruded where muscle once ruled, and he leant awkwardly to one side. And yet he was alive. Malnourished, bloody, mutilated, destroyed. Alive. A fresh set of scars told a new story, one I mourned never hearing.

He turned to the Central Guard Tower – those bastards that demanded a spectacle – defiant and triumphant. He faltered. The glimmer of feeling on his face was so fleeting, so hidden that only someone trained to find it would notice. A little opening of the mouth, widening of the eye, a second lingering too long on another. A spark of electricity in the stagnant air.

He saw me. He didn't expect me.

Why would he? What would a one-eyed, female pirate not wearing the uniform of the prisoners be doing here? Especially one he was in love with and last saw in a pool of her own blood, drifting through the ocean. Perhaps he thought that would be the last time he saw me.

No, I controlled our destiny.

The collector walked forward, skittering across the bloody corpse. He grabbed Ant's hand and thrust it upwards, right towards the dark grey reflective surface of the Central Guard Tower.

"Your victor!" he said to no one.

It was just the three of us. Not including the dead man on the ground. Ant didn't look away.

But they watched. They always watched.

The prisoner motioned for me to join the battleground but mercifully waved Ant away in dismissal. The fight wouldn't be between us. As I walked past Ant, I placed a hand on my face, slowly dragging my fingers across my cheek until they rested on my mouth. I moved my fingers downwards until only my pointer remained on my lips, then peered intensely into Ant's eye.

Shush, my finger whispered. They did not know. For if they did, they would force us to fight too. But I am here. I am here for you. And I will find you.

He said nothing, limping away. Something had harmed his left leg, and it affected his gait. He didn't dare look backwards, and it took all my might to keep my eye forward. My heart thundered at how close its counterpart stood. Ant was alive. Ant was here. My soul wanted to lurch out and follow him, but it couldn't. Not yet. I wanted to know his thoughts, I desperately wanted to breach his mind. But I couldn't.

For what man did the Ovators think I traversed the Panopticon for? Were they really so unaware? Did they really think I had just gifted myself to this prison?

A gift they couldn't return.

My boots splashed through blood as two prisoners wearing grey hauled the corpse away. The battleground smelled of his sweat. Familiar, warm, earthy. A growl vibrated through my throat. Ant was a distraction. I didn't expect to see him yet. I needed to calm my heart rate. He won his battle, and I needed to win mine, too.

"You don't have an overseer," the collector said. "So, the other chose for you."

Mercifully, they chose the bloody prisoner I had first walked past. I must have been his second battle, for he looked too weak to have won two. Already so close to losing, so close to dying. Why would they choose him? Surely by now the Ovator Guards of this level had heard whispers of the deranged woman who sought the bottom of the Panopticon. Yet, they underestimated me. Still, after everything I'd done.

My sword tingled in my hand. A magic blade. Something forbidden in such a place. I faced my opponent, focusing on little more than my steadying breath and slowing heart.

Wounds marred tired skin. The blood on his temple was yet to clot, dripping into his reddened eyes. We circled each other, this man who would die for Ovator entertainment. He surely was grateful his opponent was a woman. A woman who didn't wear a jumpsuit. He couldn't measure my strength as a colour. He would underestimate me. While he wore orange, I had killed much darker shades.

The opponent prisoner had chosen an axe as his weapon. It was a flimsy thing – a terrible choice – showing inexperience, its hilt made of plywood. He would have been better off with the avisale breastplate, since the birds seemed impervious to mortal swords. It was already a miracle that the weapon had survived a previous round. The forged steel clung ferociously to wood, splinters pricking his hands, and his perspiring already thickened the air. Those were the weaknesses to exploit.

I attacked first. My opponent had time to assess my size and my eye, but I hadn't given him an opportunity to admire my sword. I lunged forward, striking toward his shoulder. He jolted off balance, switching stance for the axe to catch my sword.

He lifted it in time. Steel bounced off steel, my blade producing a beautiful orange glow with the sparks of the force. The prisoner's eyes widened. The weapon purred in response, the sound skipping within me and out with a laugh. Another fresh droplet of blood fell into his now-widened brown eyes. He tried to blink it away, but it impaired him. My nose tickled with the scent of promised death.

Without hesitation, conserving my energy, I pulled my sword back and threw it at the prisoner. This time it cut through the belly of the handle. The steel blade thudded against the ground. I considered pulling back once more but followed through instead.

This was just my first fight, and I wouldn't waste unnecessary energy. Not when I had come so far. The blade sliced through flesh, clicking on bone. He yelped. The sound so feeble in its urgency. Already so injured, already so tired. My blade was merely an insult to his already dying body. The prisoner just hadn't realised it.

He was already dead.

"I'm sorry," I said as I hauled my sword back and slid it through his throat.

The gurgling sound rang cruel. The prisoner looked at me. He seemed so pathetically young, so unwilling to die, so unaware that a meagre death rewarded his unknown life. As though he weren't the jumpsuit he wore, but an unwritten book, a lost soul. Only a moment of recognition flashed through his chocolate-brown eyes before nothingness conquered.

Every other death seemed necessary, seemed useful. Not this one. This was a spectacle. A death designed to quench the thirst of those with power. The body thudded against the concrete, no longer the soul's vessel.

I wouldn't allow the collector to raise my hand in victory like he did Ant's.

He hadn't yet grabbed the next opponent. Maybe he expected a longer battle, a grander challenge. He was wrong. Life took years to build and sculpt, yet only seconds to destroy.

He motioned to grab my hand, and I flinched away.

"Touch me and you die," I spoke through gritted teeth.

He complied.

"Your victor." He glanced towards the Central Guard Tower and shrugged.

As the collector led me back to my practice zone, I kept looking for Ant, focused. Focused and manic. Every second in that battle was a second too long. I scanned every partition we passed, some empty, some with prisoners awaiting death, one with a prisoner missing both his eyes. My breath hitched, whistling. No Ant. When the collector dropped me off, and when Ant hadn't appeared, I pushed past the partition and ran, no longer controlled by finding Ant but consumed by it.

The partition next to mine sat empty. That prisoner died, gone in an unfortunate moment, by my blade. The burly man still waited in the front partition, but he wasn't Ant. I raced forward once more, about to flee, about to give up this stupid damned level and force my way down.

But there, where I had fallen through the hole, where the weapons master waited, there he was.

Ant.

Beautifully broken, the most wonderful sight in the most shocking of places. My breath steadied.

"What is this?" The weapons master had been too busy to notice me, scribbling down his notes, recording Ant's victory. He looked up now. "You should be fighting."

"I won." My sword dripped with the blood of my victim.

A flicker of relief floated across Ant's face – always so terrible at poker.

"I thought I told you the rules. You must win three fights! Three fights! Go back and wait for your next one."

I tried to focus on the weapons master but allowed my gaze to drift to Ant's features that silhouetted my vision. He looked at me, of course he did, and no prisoner would be suspicious for doing so. A mad woman wearing pirate clothes in a prison? Only those who held secrets wouldn't stare. It was like I gifted Antorn a sliver of home. A familiar, steady figure, in a place void of it. My eye looked at his, an offering of the ocean, before snapping back towards the weapons master.

This was stupid. Running here wasn't part of the ruse. I needed to be confident and calm, determined. The game had been so achingly slow already, I couldn't give up now, couldn't act irrationally. But there was Ant. On the same level as me, breathing the same air. We could take the weapons. We could go and – and—

Go down, only down remained.

"Three seems like a pitiful number for all I've faced," I said, stupidly invigorated by Ant's presence. For some rash reason, I wanted him to know how far I'd come.

How far I would go.

"I figured as much with that trophy jar of yours." The weapons master looked unamused, but his words caught Ant's attention. "But if you don't get back in your space, we'll all get some unwanted attention." The weapons master's voice quivered, seeking the Central Guard Tower.

I wanted to retort, let them, let them come out, let them fight me. But that wasn't strategic, and I had one more trinket. One more magic trinket that needed to be used on that very bottom level. Patience, something that waned.

"Fine," I said, willing my eye to stay on the weapons master. "Fine, I will win two more of your stupid battles."

Before burning the place down. My eye said this. My heart said this.

I looked at Ant as he looked at me. My heart stumbled. Endless words unable to be spoken, but endless words that begged to be. He'd gone to hell. I came to save him, and to doom us both.

I pivoted, walking away. Ant won his three battles. Of course, he had. He would move down. Two more fights to go, and then we'd meet again, two more, and we'd strike.

"Women," I heard the weapons master mutter to Ant.

"Sir, you have no idea." Ant chuckled.

What an oddly melodic sound in such a vile place. Laughter was like blue. I wanted to bottle it. Warmed by the noise, I returned to my partitioned zone.

My mind had set. I was no prisoner.

I didn't yield to their ridiculous rules. Three fights. Ridiculous I had even taken part in one. Ant distracted me. I didn't want to be a victor, didn't want the blessing to survive one extra level. I wouldn't win their torture. No longer a pawn in their game. I would steal it, just as I'd taken everything else in this place. What a ludicrous prize. Most prisoners were better off dead on this level than facing what came next.

The plate of gruel sat uneaten on my table, and the glass empty. I had to do it—

Had to make it worth it, make my abandonment, make leaving Navira worth it all.

0 DAYS UNTIL CAPTURE:

Ant stabbed me. He stuck his dagger in my abdomen and kicked me off the ship.

Rising embarrassment fuelled my movement towards the shore. Despite the throbbing pain and dripping blood, I was an unstoppable barrel of rage. I didn't look back. Not as Ovators seized our ship, not as a billow of smoke signalled the change of ownership. He was taken. I knew he stabbed me for that reason, for if he hadn't, I would've hopped back on that ship in an instant and been taken, too.

My blood mixed with salty seawater. It prickled. I fumed red hot — a wrathful woman. The gods created me. They pathed the way for me and Ant to meet, to fall in love, to end in tragedy. The gods didn't know what hell they'd unleashed on this world.

Mercifully, the crew had already escaped on the rowboat. Ant had begged me to go with them. Of course, I said no. He couldn't go. He needed to distract the Ovators, allowing the crew to disappear. They were after the God Killer, after all. He couldn't force me, and he didn't try to, not as he placed the satchel of our most prized magic trinkets over my neck. Not as he stabbed me and kicked me off the ship with his boot.

We had been so close to the docks. So close to making it on land, for having a tiny shred of protection around other pirates and magic-dealers. Ovators would never have been so bold outside of the open ocean. We had the God Killer, for only a minute, but we had it.

98

My journey back to the shore was dizzying. Perhaps the rowboat came to retrieve me. Perhaps Will gestured at me to slow down so he could see the damage done to my side. Ant had perfectly missed the organs. The lateral, lower quadrant of my abdomen wounded. Mother, I was so mad.

I dripped with ocean water and blood as I stormed into the tavern lining the shoreline. The tavern so frequented by transient pirates.

Navira gasped when I entered, as though she'd seen a drenched ghost. I was equally shocked to see her behind the bar, drying a glass with a tattered rag. It had been weeks since we'd seen each other. In a peasant costume, her light had dimmed.

"I thought we gave you enough coin not to work?" I paused, the squeak of my boots catching against the sticky tavern ground. Navira's lip tugged upwards, then stopped. "Is that a knife—"

"Dagger," I corrected as Will and Daphne flung open the tavern doors and entered behind me. "Don't change the subject."

Navira stared at the dagger. "You've been gone for weeks. It ran out. Is that—"

"Ant's." I rolled my eye. "Yes, it is."

Navira ushered me – dripping with water – Daphne and Will through the tavern and up the rickety staircase to her room. We creaked loudly, the wood sagging with fervent steps. She had questions: where Ant was, what the hell happened, why he stabbed me, but my fury paralysed her.

We had left Navira and a bag of mostly counterfeit coins before starting our journey to the God Killer. The tavern owner was meant to use our payment to allow her lodging, not for labour.

She had grown so much in the years with us into a wonderful, gifted woman. Her hair still shone silver, long and straight it shimmered in the sun. Her pale skin at odds with the pirate life she lived. She was a dreamer, not a pirate. I was so grateful she was here, not still on the ship where she didn't belong, where we forced her to fit. Maybe now she could achieve her dreams, or at least find them.

When we crouched within her small living quarters, walls covered in illustrations, I dropped the satchel with a thud and began searching, separating the useful magic from the useless. I already knew where they'd take Ant.

That desperation still fuelled me.

I had been so distracted by Ant that I hadn't absorbed my surroundings in my last fight. There was no time for distraction now. I could just glimpse the shadowed hole to the next level down at the very edge of the curve.

So close to us, me and the brutish, oversized prisoner from the very first partition. My next opponent. So close to the exit down. Here, he sought to win his freedom. Not I. Freedom was a false promise.

The blood painting the ground had been mopped with a dry rag, leaving a thin smear layered atop a history of battles. Another layer in the unending brutality of this asinine level.

Ant was with me in spirit, and in eye. I didn't plan to return to my partition. The jar sat squished against my breasts once more, cuddled by the bindings. I tired of their games.

The prisoner wore a blood-orange jumpsuit, close to Ant's shade. My first matchup had been a harmless test. This was the true battle. Where the Ovator Guards meant to do me harm. They tired of watching me succeed, wanting to kill me quickly now.

They still underestimated me

We faced each other. The prisoner loomed over me, as tall as Ant, and considered me over a large, curled nose, his bald head covered in tiny scars, eyes blackened by determination, breath thick with heat. His enormous hands could crush my skull with minimal exertion. I couldn't rely on my strength, for I had none.

Not yet.

The Ovator Guards must have known about my magic trinkets, yet they still allowed me to have them.

The fight began. The prisoner wielded a rounded club. Nothing sharp, but everything powerful. He flung it towards me. I jumped back, rummaging through my velvet medicine bag, careful to avoid the two black pills, and picked up the red pill. It already hummed. I swallowed it quickly.

I may lack strength, but I had fought against strength. Studied it, adapted to it. Ant. And Ant was much cleverer than this prisoner in front of me, and I was much faster than Ant.

And now, as I felt the red medicine unleashed in my blood, felt the prickle of fire throughout my veins as it shot through every inch of me, now I was feral. Warm. Full.

More than alive. I was a fucking god.

0 DAYS UNTIL CAPTURE:

"Willem, please!" I cursed out, the contents of the wet satchel strewn across Navira's wobbly wooden desk. I pushed her illustrations away in my haste. The action would leave me feeling guilty, but I was too irrational to care.

Will shrugged, attempting to bandage my freshly stitched side. The bandage sat loosely against salted, damp skin. He knew not to challenge me, and when I snarled at him and Daphne to leave, they complied.

"What are you doing?" Navira stood behind me, her shaking hands anchored on her hips.

"I need to decide what to bring," I snapped back. The monocular, the flash ball, the bag of magic detectors. I separated the different colours of medicine from each other, curating a specific cocktail based on the tales of the Panopticon. Think. But I couldn't. I couldn't think. What was true? What was rumoured? Think.

"Please stop," Navira whispered. "I know you love him. I love him too, but please stop—"

"Navira, please." I picked up two red pills and shone them up towards the light. One was translucent. That one.

"Ant told you never to take that one," Navira said. "He said it would turn you mad."

"Well, you've got to be a little mad to break into the Panopticon." My voice was barely recognisable, like a stranger on my lips.

"No!" She shook. "No, you can't. You'll die. You'll both die."

If I were more rational, perhaps the whimper in Navira's voice would pause me. She loved Ant. It differed from the love I felt, but she loved him too. She didn't want him to die. She would mourn him.

But I wasn't rational, and I had curated my concoction. I looked down at the pills placed on top of the pouch. Five in total. It would do.

"Farrah, please." Navira rested a hand on my shoulder. "Please, I can't lose you too. I can't."

But she couldn't stop me. I didn't answer her as her hazel eyes met my blue one. I was going to speak, to bridge the emotional gap we had made until—

"Farrah!" Daphne called.

I shrugged Navira off and hurried downstairs. My crew wanted orders. I dismissed them all. Told them to leave. Navira would stay, Navira would start her own life. I would go alone. Maybe we would meet again, maybe in the next life, but at least they still had lives to live. Mine was now borrowed.

There were no goodbyes.

When I returned upstairs, Navira had placed the medicine pills in the velvet pouch for me. I took it as silent confirmation. Some silent act of understanding, that she understood. It was so much more than that.

The red pill was certainly a foolish choice, but coupled with a dozen other foolish choices, it almost felt logical. Ant procured the red medicine years before we met. He had claimed it was rare, the only one remaining, a piece of a seer's soul, driven to madness before death. It gave its user increased senses, but an unquenchable blood thirst. Like the red magic of level four, but condensed omnipotence. My heart thrummed in a rhythm unsung by the gods themselves, my breath threatened to turn into a growl, emboldened by waves of electricity that pushed from my toes to my throat, to my tingling hands.

It would cause a shocking hangover when it wore off, but I had planned to be dead long before that.

The prisoner paused, club raised, as he surveyed me. My skin turned translucent, veins thick and bold like tree roots. My insides burned. Fire boiled my blood, but instead of pain, I became the flame, seeking to burn. I didn't know what he saw when he looked in my eye, but his club stumbled down, just a fraction.

I moved impossibly fast, my blade working in quick succession, leaving shallow cuts over the prisoner's body. Some cut little further than the cotton of his jumpsuit, but others tore at flesh and turned orange cotton crimson. The prisoner bashed his club against my shoulder. A crack resounded. My body didn't feel. It no longer felt anything, as though rage consumed every molecule of pain that attempted to invade me. My mind understood the injury, but the magic soothed a silenced release.   I controlled the magic within, and it burned deep.

I stuck my blade through his right forearm as he flung his fist into my cheek. Another crack, the crunching of bone fragments, but no pain. The blow sent me tumbling backwards, but I just laughed through blood-stained teeth. A boiled metallic scent whispered from nose to mind.

The Ovator Guards certainly believed I was seconds from death. In fact, the collector had left to get the next contestants. Now was my chance. This battle wasn't my fate. I had no qualms about the man in front of me, the man that now raised his club to swing downwards in a final, fatal blow. We were both hostages in a game I no longer wished to play.

I slid underneath him, squeaking across slick concrete, then flung my body forward into a roll. I ran. I kept running. Forward. I could feel the prisoner staring at my back, heard the yells as the collector returned with the next contestant, but I still ran. No one could stop me, no obstacle, just me and that hole.

I didn't bother detecting magic.

I was the magic as I barrelled down headfirst. The ultimate level: level one.

And so, it ends.

9. Level One

Level one exuded its distinction through many sources. Everything differed – the air, the walls, the smell, my body. My mind.

The Central Guard Tower watched me fall.

They watched. They always watched.

The level hummed, buzzing with power, slashing through the veil of my drug-hazed brain. The fire festered within me so much stronger now. It distracted, bouncing off my mind's walls. Of course, the magic lied, waning, but down here, there was little time for truth.

The walls shifted from pure-orange clay to metal threaded throughout organic grooves. Tiny pipes twisted over the clay like tree roots. Pipes thickened and sloshed until leading towards one undeniable path.

That one pipe carried from this level to the top.

I couldn't see its source from where I stood, for it sprawled across the entire level. But I knew.

That was it, water powered the Panopticon. Of all the power sources they could choose in a barren land with a bleeding sun, they chose water. A hydropower prison, perhaps a gift from the Rain God, or the Sea God. The prisoners starved and died of thirst, and yet the liquid that could grow crops, that could quench their needs, kept the torture powered.

The pure hatred wasn't lost on me.

Level one stretched much wider than the previous levels, its depth oddly disconcerting after such consistency. My eye thrummed with change. It had to be grander, for the rumours rang true. Not only was level one the power source, but where they created the pets.

The prisoners down here didn't win freedom, nor their death. The prisoners survived magic, famine and plague, they bested three of their fellow men, not for any prize.

They won the privilege of becoming pets of the gods.

Circular cages sat throughout the level. Cages within a cage, so small, prisoners couldn't fully lie down. They had to hug the bars to rest. White bone bars wrapped around each prisoner, enclosed by a steel roof. The cages didn't reach the ceiling, instead, adorned with polished skulls.

It was a travesty against mortals not to burn their remains and set their souls free. The prisoners were never freed. They either died and became décor or were granted agonising immortality. A lifetime of being a pet.

Finally, as a witness to level one, I expected the Central Guard Tower to act, and yet, they still watched.

The closest caged prisoners were the nearest to a full transformation. Their forms shifted dependent on the bids of the gods. I passed the first prisoner, painted with golden feathers. His mouth still fleshy, but now painfully stretched in the shape of a beak. His left arm fell like a limp, dead snake, and he wore the Sun God's mark on his feathered chest.

I faltered. I wanted to end it for him, end the suffering. As I walked past, I imagined sticking my sword through the cage and snagging him before he reached unimaginable immortality. But I kept moving. Whatever gods wanted this man, I wasn't ready to catch their eyes.

Who watched me now? Did any? The Ovator Guards didn't have direct access to their gods. Yet they still committed these atrocities to their fellow man to appease petty gods. They sickened me. Pious pricks.

The next prisoner fared no better. He lingered almost fully a pet, save for his left leg. His right leg had transformed into a wooden stick, and he leaned on the last of his mortality. His upper body was bulbous, soft, pillowy flesh, coated in a light blue sheen. Only grey eyes bore impermanence on his face, and he had no nose to sniff up his tears. Leaving him pained me, and I made a wordless promise that it would be worth it.

My body pulsed with the effects of the red magic pill, a purring at the back of my head, demanding more violence. As I stepped, I floated. The prisoners blended in, frozen between a state of mortal and creature. Eventually, I didn't look at their forms. The serpents, rabbits, beaks, wings, feathers. Just their eyes. Not Ant. Not Ant. Again and again, the eyes that stared back at me, that pleaded to be released, weren't Ant.

Soon.

Soon, I would burn this place down.

This was why I knew I would die. Why I contentedly embraced death, comforted that Ant would die too. He would be better off dead than an eternal pet to a god he despised. This was the level to disrupt – the level to destroy.

I subtly clutched the last magic trinket on my belt, for the Central Guard Tower surely watched every move. Maybe curiosity still stopped them, or they awaited the orders of a god. They let me move.

I thought of my goodbye to Navira. So bitter, heavy with unspoken words.

0 DAYS UNTIL CAPTURE:

As I rummaged through the magic trinkets on Navira's desk, I knew I needed to find the Panopticon. Ant had told me the stories, all the ones he knew. Between our battles, between our lovemaking, he bared everything. His vendetta, his fears, his hope and his pain. His quest to kill a god. The quest now dead. Rumours of the Panopticon spread across the entire world, whispered between ships, between pirates, given life. Yet no one knew where they came from.

No one escaped, he had told me, not even his father. But rumours had.

"I am coming with you," Navira begged me.

"No." I didn't look. "You will only get in the way."

Navira retreated. Her hands clenched as my eye drifted to her. Her silver hair flashed grey, hazel eyes swimming in translucent tears. Words formed in her mind but got lost on her lips. Ever the dreamer, but this nightmare was real.

She couldn't stop me.

"Please, at least let me help you find it." She grabbed my arm, but I yanked it away.

It was for her own good that she wasn't part of my death. I wanted to hold her, feel her warmth, and say goodbye. I wanted to tell her I loved her, that finding her was the best thing that ever happened to Ant and me. But now she had to discover the life she dreamed of living. Without us, she'd be free.

"No, Navira."

I left enough magic trinkets for Navira to sell and live comfortably for a while. Perhaps use the coin to find a ship, illustrate a book, explore a fantastical world. She was smart enough to understand this, smart enough that there was no point in telling her. I didn't want to be nice. She needed to let me go.

All I mustered before my voice croaked and my eye leaked was, "Goodbye."

I didn't look at her. I didn't hear from her. Never again. Not as I ate and trained and fought my way through the world until I found the Panopticon. Not as I commissioned the meek man to craft me a plague mask, or as I hid on pirate and Ovator ships to get to the Panopticon. Any time I heard whispers of a silver-haired woman, I made myself believe it was her. Made myself believe she had left and sought an adventure. It propelled me forward. I hoped she found something to let me go.

She deserved a better world than the one she'd gotten.

Movement.

The Central Guard Tower.

I faltered in my step, a fragment of that red magic pill waning. Something changed. I examined the Central Guard Tower but only my reflection stared back. I looked horrendous. Torn, bloody, dirty, sweaty. Broken. Frenzied. Like my mortality had caught in a temporary limbo, waiting to be unleashed.

My once-cream tunic had browned with beast blood, prisoner blood and my own blood. Mercifully, the black pants hid whatever damage lay underneath. Mania owned my eye. Whilst still blue, red magic clouded the white. Energy pulsed as a trick, and I had little left until the truth triumphed. It was why I had to take the pill carefully, for when it faded, the soft crunch underneath my cheek would surely bite through the last of my sanity.

That fucking prisoner had to get one good swing in.

It felt like I traversed the entire floor of the Panopticon until I found him.

Ant.

So many caged prisoners, so many captured souls. He sat in one of the last cages. A hanging white bulb brightly lit the cage, as if he were art on display. His expression seemed peculiar, unreadable, as he leaned on the white bone bars. A mix of uncertainty, hope, and trepidation. In fact, it took him several moments to gather the strength to gaze at me with his one remaining brown eye.

I did it. I finally found him.

My hands grasped the bones of the cage. They were smooth, cold to the touch, and void of any scent. I didn't care that I leaned my head against prisoner's bones. Cared about little more than being here, in this moment, with him.

Ant stood and limped forward. There had been no bids, and his body remained wholly his own. He didn't speak, resting his forehead against mine, the only sound a quiver that vibrated up his throat. We were both dirty, sticky with sweat and blood, but a brief flicker of energy pulsed between us. There was no greater feeling than his flesh pressed against mine, even separated by bone bars. It was what I had moved for, what had propelled me through the seven levels of hell.

Together again at last. So many stories rested in those weeks apart. It could be just like those days in bed recounting our histories, tracing their outlines on our bodies, but we no longer had time. Though time here stagnated, I was determined to stop it.

Finally, he said, "I both cannot believe you are here, and cannot believe it took you so long." His voice was so hoarse, it almost sounded unfamiliar, but mother, it was such a delicious gift.

I grinned at this. "Next time you're abducted, leave directions first."

He smirked. "You had nothing better to do than save a dead man?"

"I couldn't let you become their pet."

Ant flinched, but before my skin missed his touch, he lifted a hand and rested it on my cheek. Particles of loose bone shifted as his fingers brushed against my skin, yet there was no pain. His touch, it broke through it all.

"I'm sorry about your eye," I murmured as I considered the blood crusting in his socket.

He laughed manically. "Your cheek is putty, shoulder limp, and you look like you just ran through a magic whirlpool, yet you worry about my eye?"

Our bond broke as I reached into my tunic and pulled out the glass jar, placing it in Ant's hand. "I'm fine."   I was.

He looked down at the glass. A man wasn't meant to gaze into his own eye so easily.

"I would suggest we find a healer to put it back, but something tells me this isn't a rescue mission."

I tapped my belt and placed a hand over my last magic trinket. Even though black leather covered it, Ant knew by its shape what lay underneath. His breath hitched.

"No one survives the Panopticon," I said, our eyes meeting.

This was what the Ovator Guards waited for. They wanted to know who I was foolish enough to traverse the entire prison for, who owned my heart, and possibly, whose to break to break me.

Not only the Ovator Guards, but the gods too.

Everyone watched, and I tired of it.

The ground rumbled beneath my feet. I turned from Ant at the vibrations, eye fixated on the Central Guard Tower. It shuddered with so much movement that my reflection shook back at me as the magic inside me dimmed.

Not yet, I growled. I still needed it, we still needed time.

"How do I get you out?" I faced Ant once more, fingers exploring the bleached bone bars, achingly aware the Guard Tower may open any second.

Ant looked upwards at his cage's metal roof. He looked down at the concrete ground. Then, with a furrowed brow, he looked at the bones that lined the cage before finally resting on my sword.

"Remember the first night we met?" Ant didn't wait for an answer. "When you commandeered my ship and slept so soundly in my quarters? I was going to kill you, I really was. But the sword by your head, the sword that you slept with, carved by the volcano. It wasn't just a powerful blade. It told me as much about its magic as it did yours. Only a powerful pirate could wield such a thing. So, wield it, my cyclone, and let's end this."

Bone against steel, I suppressed a laugh. What pretty, ornate cages. What pitiful protection. Ant pressed against the rounded backside of the cage. I raised my sword, hilt humming red, and embers of lava flittered through it and into my arms. The magic still throbbed through me like a circuit, waiting for its heat to be unleashed. With a roar, before the Ovator Guards stopped me, I used all my remaining might to slice through the bones and carve them. I did it again, and again, until the bones collapsed in a splintered mess.

All Ant needed to do was kick the cage, and it came crumbling down. He was free.

Perhaps it was folly for us to embrace. Perhaps we should be more worried about the approaching guards, the shouts, the movements. His lips found mine in an instant, hand gripping the underside of my chin. We smelt terrible – but wonderful – like familiarity perfumed us, the connection a miracle despite our meagre odds. Magic rushed onto my tongue as it carried to his mouth. He was warm, like a fire heating its home. He kept my heart beating, and dimmed the noise, the footsteps, the gods.

I was home and ready to die. Every movement, every death, every drop of sweat had brought me here. Brought me to him. To my heart, to my soul. He bit down gently on my bottom lip before ending the kiss.

The first Ovator Guard struck us the moment we parted. The guards wore white from their heads to their toes, and helmets obscured their identities. They mimicked the bleached shade of the bones surrounding us. Unlike the Ovators who ruled over the lands wearing white silk, these didn't wish to be known. Pious pricks. No longer watching. For once, they joined.

Five guards attacked, and we had only one weapon. My sword. Mercifully, Ant found the energy to face one with desperate, bare hands. One lunged at Antorn, another at me, weapons clasped in white-gloved hands. The Ovator Guards carried humming batons.

Fucking magic.

I grunted as my sword collided with the baton of the first Ovator Guard. It practically magnetised, driving my blade backwards at the contact. I groaned as shockwaves raced up my injured shoulder, thunder booming through the length of my veins. The magic pill thinned. We didn't have time.

Ant separated another guard from his weapon. He had only seconds until the next leapt upon him. He grabbed the Ovator Guard's head and slammed it into the concrete. It cracked – a force so strong it pushed through his helmet. The crack turned damp as blood seeped free. The next Ovator Guard slammed his baton into Ant's stomach before he had time to fully turn. Ant collapsed with a howl.

"Ant!" I called.

I was so distracted, I didn't see the baton from the next Ovator Guard as it hit my side. The pain penetrated through the numbing red magic. Prickles of magic left the curve of the baton and embedded deep within the skin of my side. It didn't relent. It just built.

We were outnumbered. I stuck my sword into another Ovator Guard's shoulder, where his leather uniform was weak with thread. He backed away, blood mixing pink with the leather. Ant stood, though the same pain that thundered through my side surely crippled him. A few more hits and it would consume us, and the jolts would cause our hearts to stop. This wasn't a winning battle, not with these rules.

"What are you waiting for?" Ant roared at me.

I had shown him what awaited the Panopticon, what needed to be embedded within that Central Guard Tower, the vessel that could move a flame upwards, that waited to burn a prison down. If I only had the chance to free the last magic trinket—

There. Was it a mirage? In my haste to free Ant, I didn't see. Not only did the pipe that connected the power and water from this level to the very top sit in the corner of my vision, but next to it – a door.

A metal door. Made of the same material as the Central Guard Tower, but within the clay wall bulbs illuminated it like the hope of a sunrise.

Some legends were wrong. Indeed, this being one of them. Legend had it that there was no escaping the

Panopticon. And yet, a door existed on the very bottom level. A door that built optimism.

My sword met the stomach of the next Ovator Guard, though it didn't pierce through his thick uniform. As he fumbled backward, I gripped the leather fabric wrapped around the last useful magical trinket and pulled it off with one swift move.

We never knew when a magic bomb would come in handy. It felt somewhat tasteless, particularly for magic-dealers who appreciated a home. Especially for pirates. Surely, it was bad luck to have a bomb on board a wooden ship. But what better use for a bomb than to blow up the fucking Panopticon?

I unwrapped the leather. The bomb circular, covered in small, raised grooves. It was not coloured. In fact, it devoured colour.

Ant glanced towards me, feverish, panting, lips dripping with blood. He saw the bomb in my hand, then followed my eye to where it rested on the door. We both needed no words. Several more Ovator Guards left the Central Guard Tower, and surely more would arrive.

Drown it.

I thought back to that one dying prisoner. Thought of the request at odds with the bomb on my person. I had planned to blow the place up, fling the thing into the Central Guard Tower. How could a bomb drown a prison in the desert? Now, I knew.

'Magic bomb' was the colloquial term used to describe the trinket – yet it operated as so much more. It collected atoms that tore and released, multiplying. So, in theory, the bomb would attach to the Central Guard Tower, exploding metal like shrapnel until the whole place caught on fire with friction. For a pipe, however, the outer shell would shatter, and water would replicate up the vessel and through the prison until magic waned and failed.

Ant and I both stood up and ran in synchronised movements. He reached the door first, though his limp slowed us down. With great fortune, it wasn't locked. As he yanked it open and collapsed within, as the Ovator Guards chased me, time seemed to slow, until it stopped.

It stopped as I flung the magic bomb onto the pipe, the throw perfect in execution. It stuck, the magic humming through me made sure of it. It stopped as I slid the remaining steps, as the air stilled, then floated inwards like a giant wave.

Time didn't move as the world exploded, as magic and air that had been trapped for a millennium unleashed around the bottom level of the Panopticon in a bellowing cry. It didn't move as water erupted from the roof to the walls, to that central pipe, carrying water up and throughout the seven levels of hell. It didn't move as I finally slid through the door and Ant closed it.

Without the pipe, without a way up, the level may have contained the magic, taking Ovator Guards and pets, perhaps resulting in a slow implosion. But with it came movement greater than any rogue wave. We couldn't see what happened, what destruction the magic bomb gifted. We could only hope that the incomplete pets received some peace.

A wave crashed against the door with a shudder, pinning us within, signifying the climax of the bomb. No mortal would be strong enough to pry the door open with the growing flood. We were safe. The Panopticon was not. The magic and water roared a shrill death shriek, despite the door cocooning us. A small opening at its bottom began letting in tiny trickles of water.

No light greeted us, for it was no corridor, and no exit. It was a room. A room, it seemed, without purpose, taunting us with its emptiness. The only light flared from my sword, producing a red, golden glow that struggled against the darkness. That brief flicker of hope died as we both clawed at the walls, desperately trying to find some sort of exit. Another door, a secret, a protruding gap in the clay. Anything. But it was too dark, and there was nothing but the natural curves of the clay.

My movement increased with the whispers of waning hope, though my legs numbed with the dimming red magic. No, this door wouldn't fool us. There had to be more. The clay was moist but solid. Magic held tricks, but I didn't expect one in such poor taste from the Panopticon.

The laugh that escaped Ant was manic with every emotion. The floor vibrated from the destruction outside.

I had done it. I had found Ant, destroyed the Panopticon, and taken it down with us. The destruction crescendoed to a roar outside the room. We heard as gasps and screams turned into gurgles and chokes. So, why did it feel so bittersweet?

"Thank you." Ant grabbed my hands from the masquerading room's wall. "Thank you for rescuing me."

This was always the plan. To die. We were destined to end in tragedy. Those who dealt magic by sea were the most cursed.

As the red pill faded, the pain in my shoulder grew. My cheek ached. My leg thrummed with the reminder of the perfect circle gifted from the manic prisoner on the red magic level. Bruises, cuts, boils and blood covered my body, and the death of several prisoners had crusted under my fingernails. I was so painfully hungry, so desperately thirsty, with barely any skin left that was solely mine. But a curious calm washed over me. I dropped Ant's hand only to fumble open the velvet pouch and pull free the last two useful pills. The two black pills. The death pills.

Maybe the Enchantress knew it would come to this. Maybe this was our prize for destroying the Panopticon, a final fuck you to the god that abandoned her. Whatever the reason, it was our destiny.

I placed one pill in Ant's hand. Mine trembled. His stilled. He gave me strength. We were exhausted, so tired of fighting. Together, we raised the black pills up to our mouths in mirrored actions. It smelled curiously warm, spicy, almost citrusy. A pleasant smell for something that would bring us death, nothing like the scent the pills wafted in the Enchantress' house all those moons ago. Maybe it told us we were ready, soothing us into death. Not to fear it.

"Did you think, all those years ago, when my crew captured your ship, that we'd end up here?" I asked, voice shaky.

Antorn smiled. "The destination is not ideal. But I loved every moment of our journey." He brushed my cheek. "Every moment, Farrah. I mean it. I wouldn't trade even a breath with you for a peaceful life alone."

"Let's be honest, Ant. We weren't built for peace."

My smile faltered, the pill in my hand cold and lifeless. We didn't need more words. We needed to act.

"Thank you." He breathed out, his hand brushed my neck, before clutching my hand, and I understood the weight of his words, the unspoken relief I had gifted by rescuing him.

I would do it again, and again, and again. I would live in a constant loop of death and pain and the seven levels of hell if it always brought us to this moment, together.

Ant and I swallowed our pills, hands gripped tightly. I wanted nothing more than to touch his skin, for our bodies to finish the stories they told together. Not his end. Not mine. Ours. A duology completed. Despite the darkness, despite the sound of destruction around us, I knew.

He watched. His one golden brown eye stared into my blue one.

A destiny of tragedy, taken back.

The Pirate and the Pet's Curse

By Katherine Clark

Chapter one preview:

CHAPTER 1

Nightmares

The moment finally arrived. The moment Navira had been waiting for.

It had only been a few weeks, but every night she dreamed she'd see her family soon, and every morning, she'd wake with brilliant, unyielding hope.

The tavern door opened, then slammed shut, stealing sunlight and extinguishing Navira's optimism in a force that resounded across the dark wooden walls.

Her grin twisted into a frown.

Liquid pooled at the tavern's entrance as Farrah dripped, drenched in seawater – and blood. She raised a soaked hand, flinging water that blended into the sticky tavern floor.

If Navira weren't so worried about her injured guardian, she'd fret that the tavern owner Jeffrey would return from the docks before she had the chance to mop the mess.

Weeks had passed since Antorn and Farrah had abandoned her at the nameless town's tavern. At first, she bought the privilege of living above the decapitated dwelling. Then, she earned her housing by bartending. It wasn't the worst job, but she wasn't very good at it.

The tavern usually bustled with customers, but trade had slowed. Ever since Farrah and Antorn had dropped her off, according to Jeffrey. According to Jeffrey, her guardians were to blame for a lot that went wrong in the nameless town.

Navira leaned behind the bar, expecting Antorn to stroll into the tavern, muttering curses at his lover, but he never did.

When Farrah trudged closer, Navira narrowed her gaze, recognising the blood's origin.

A thinly handled dagger protruded from Farrah's abdomen.

"I thought we gave you enough coin not to work?" Farrah frowned. Her hand hovered over her stomach, inches from the bulging blade.

"Is that a knife—"

"Dagger," Farrah corrected. "Don't change the subject."

The dagger submerged deep within wet linen and flesh, dipping to the ground, as if gravity bested the skin-hugging metal.

Navira wondered if the dagger met the other side. "You've been gone for weeks. It ran out. Is that—"

"Ant's." Farrah rolled her one remaining blue eye, the other long ago stolen. "Yes, it is."

The pirate who had never strolled through the tavern door had stabbed his lover. It made no sense. Navira blinked away the lie, but the crimson truth remained.

Antorn and Farrah had rescued Navira from her burned-down village, Utorpa, when she was a teenager. Once a picturesque village, Navira had seen little of it. Kept in a cage, she hadn't even witnessed the surrounding sea. When drought destroyed crops, when flames ravaged the villagers, Navira rejoiced. Just a teenager, but so ready to die. The air had stripped moisture, and buildings collapsed into soot and ashen corpses.

Roaring fire stole everything – everyone – but forgot her.

They'd spent the last half a decade sailing the seas together, procuring rare magic trinkets, until her guardians abandoned her to chase the worst kind of magic – a weapon.

The God Killer.

Had they finally found it?

God Killer thoughts rippled through Navira, shoulders tensing at the violence the blade promised.

She blinked back to reality, willing the memories away. The tavern hadn't opened, and she'd been pottering, preparing for the day's trade. Citrus fruit waited uncut on an orange-stained chopping board as she rushed to Farrah.

The tavern door opened once more, but instead of a looming brutish pirate, Willem and Daphne burst inside.

Their faces told delicate stories of misfortune.

Shipmates for over a decade, Daphne was Farrah's navigator. Usually marked by a pensive smile, Daphne grimaced, clutching a pill-shaped golden pendant hanging from her neck. Golden jewellery adorned her dark skin. Some trinkets, some containing power in memories.

Unlike Farrah's dripping form, Daphne didn't wear the ocean, nor did Will.

Will, the ship's healer, had no voice – it had long been stolen, but Navira understood his purpose as he scurried to Farrah, pushing brittle hair from his face, gesturing for her to sit down.

"Let's go upstairs," Navira said, locking the tavern door. "If Jeffrey sees the tavern covered in blood again, he'll actually kick me out."

***

Blood and seawater dyed the towels a dusty pink while Will finished stitching Farrah's wound. As Navira clutched the soiled towels, Farrah tucked her shirt into her breast bindings, Will wrapping a bandage around her waist.

Farrah and Daphne whispered fragmented truths through grunts, quips, and protests.

Ovators had stormed their ship, the *Blue Abyss*, and they'd captured Antorn and the God Killer.

They'd found the God Killer.

It couldn't be. The weapon had proved elusive for years. Yet they'd had it. For just a moment.

And Antorn was on his way to eternal imprisonment in the Panopticon. Never to see the sun again. Navira couldn't imagine living without light. Yet Ovators were renowned for their torture and depravity.

Ovators, the pious pricks that governed the lands, acted as unofficial mouthpieces to the gods. The self-appointed rulers, mortals deciding the wishes of gods, and oppressing to justify it. Ovators falsified power, controlling townspeople with the threat of vengeful gods. When young, Navira believed the threat. Now she understood its limitations. The gods didn't speak to the Ovators, and the townspeople feared a power they didn't understand.

An Ovator purchased Navira when she was young, so she knew of their portrayed superior morality but also deep selfishness. Most importantly, they didn't appreciate others trying to kill their gods.

She swallowed more questions as Farrah swatted Will's hand away.

"Will, please!"

The mute healer shrugged as he tightened the bandage, sighing. The bandage drooped, but it would prevent infection.

There wasn't enough space in the room above the tavern for all four of them. Frozen by unwanted truth, Navira lingered at the doorway, with one foot on the rickety step. Both Daphne and Will crouched to fit.

As if noticing this, Farrah turned to Daphne, wincing as her midsection twisted. "Leave us, please."

"Farrah—" Daphne warned before she pinched the bridge of her nose. "Fine."

Too overwhelmed for dissent, the two pirates left.

Trinkets from Farrah's brown satchel lay strewn across Navira's wooden desk, dampening her new artwork. She went to retrieve her illustrations, but Farrah flung them to the ground instead.

Navira recognised many of the trinkets – the pink tube, mirror, spinning disc. These were the most valuable, rarest magic trinkets.

Antorn had been taken and so had the ship. The truth swirled like an intangible impossibility.

Eternal, violent imprisonment stole his future.

"What are you doing?" Navira asked, anxiety vibrating through hands anchored on her hips.

"I need to decide what to take."

Farrah created two piles, sliding across the golden monocular, then an illuminated fuzzy ball, then a colourless sphere. A manic hand danced above the trinkets, and she pushed a dripping raven curl from her face, growling as the unruly hair struggled free once more.

"Where's the concealment paste?" Farrah grunted. "Fine. Never mind."

Next, she emptied a velvet pouch. Medicines poured out, releasing a flurry of intoxicating, herbal scents. Elusive properties perfumed the pills, and Navira simply stared as Farrah shifted a handful to one side.

Something brewed within Farrah's one wrathful blue eye, and whatever it was, Navira swallowed a sense of unavoidable doom. Now wasn't the time for rash decisions.

Antorn had been taken to the Panopticon, facing eternal torture.

And if Farrah's movements told Navira anything, her guardian aimed to join him.

"Please stop," Navira begged. "I know you love him, I love him too, but please stop—"

"Navira, please." Farrah raised two red pills to the light. One was translucent.

Navira recognised the magic pill. Antorn had sourced it long ago. It held a piece of a seer's soul, though he hadn't dared use it, claiming the magic destroyed a mortal's sanity. The pill would be immeasurably valuable, but he didn't want the power in unworthy hands. It made the user confident, strong, like death incarnate, but only for a fraction of time.

He claimed he'd only ever take the medicine if he was sure he'd die after.

"Ant told you never to take that one," Navira cried. "He said it would turn you mad."

"Well, you've got to be a little mad to break into the Panopticon."

The words stagnated in the air as all Navira's fears came to fruition.

Ovators and their lesser kin, the Ovator Guards, ran the fabled Panopticon prison. It held the evilest souls, but also those caught dealing magic. For Ovators, magic was for the gods, and anyone who possessed magic trinkets deserved death for their heresy.

Half of what Navira knew about the Panopticon came from her Ovator. The Panopticon served as a bedtime story between confinement, designed to keep her pliant.

'Don't do that, pet, otherwise I'll send you to the Panopticon.'

The other half came from Antorn and Farrah. The Panopticon was a punishment for those who dared to demand freedom. Between the two conflicting versions, so utterly at odds, Navira never knew who to believe. Regardless, the malevolent prison promised only death.

And Antorn, her sweet, kind guardian, was on his way there.

Words failed her as Farrah shifted pills beside the black velvet pouch. Two of them Navira recognised, and they terrified her more than the red pill.

The death pills.

No.

It had seemed like a cruel joke that the Enchantress – the woman dripping dark magic without a known source – gifted pills to steal life. Now, they purred like an inevitability.

Navira searched for words, actions, anything to stop Farrah from leaving. Images of white walls, mansions, and cages affronted her. Without them, it would all return. Without them, she'd be alone.

"Farrah, please," Navira begged, gripping Farrah's shoulder. "Please, I can't lose you too. I can't."

Something flickered in Farrah's eye – a fragment of worry, a shade that betrayed underlying emotions. It built hope. Maybe Navira could use it—

"Farrah!" Daphne called, peering up the narrow staircase, crouching into view. Farrah shrugged off Navira's hand, thundered down the stairs, and barked orders at the crew.

Her voice echoed as Navira stood alone, staring at the black velvet pouch.

A terrible idea formed, and her trembling hands began thumbing through the pills. Propelled by magic, no ocean could destroy the power within them. Tartness wafted as she separated the two black pills from the others. They rested atop an illustration Farrah hadn't thrown onto the ground – a large, glowing orange planet with rings. Incomplete, and now coated in water that leaked colour from page.

Angry, unwilling goodbyes carried up the stairs.

If Navira was going to act, it had to be now.

The pills hummed in her fist as she crept towards her bedside table, opening the creaky drawer to reveal a grey box with a flimsy lid. She opened it, exposing dozens of black pills. Her seasickness

126

medicine. Funny, they never appeared menacing, but in the same room as the death pills, she almost cowered.

She plucked two pills, closed the drawer, and returned to her table. With palms open, comparing the two black pills, the differences materialised. But – she alternated closing each fist – without its counterpart, similarities blended. Both black, both rounded, both humming with a source of magic.

The tapping of footsteps climbing the stairs hastened her movements.

By the time Farrah returned, Navira had placed her seasickness tablets into the velvet pouch with the others and pulled the string tight.

As Farrah approached the table, she nodded at the closed bag. For Farrah, the action might have appeared a plea for collaboration. For Navira, it simply hid her deception. Her breath released the moment she realised her betrayal went unnoticed.

Farrah clipped the trinkets onto her utility belt. The monocular, the fuzzy ball, the trinket bomb – which Navira regretted not throwing out the window – the magic detectors, the dagger coated in blood, and the medicine pouch.

Desperation swelled, but words stuck to the back of Navira's throat. The death pills may no longer end Farrah's life, but that deception only destroyed one form of death. And at the Panopticon, several others remained.

Unfortunately for Navira, she was never good with words. Or actions. Or thoughts.

"I am coming with you," she begged, the only words she could manage.

With a pause, Farrah shifted, eye downcast.

"No. You'll only get in the way."

Tears welled in Navira's eyes.

"Please, at least let me help you find it." She gripped Farrah's arm.

"No, Navira." Farrah yanked her arm away before approaching the door. Her hand pressed against the doorframe, and though she didn't look over her shoulder, her voice betrayed a tremble. "Goodbye."

Farrah's footsteps faded as the door clicked open and closed. Waiting with a thundering heart, Navira remained.

Perhaps Farrah would return, realise her folly. She would come back. She wouldn't leave.

Minutes passed, then an hour.

Gone.

Farrah wasn't coming back. Navira exhaled through the panic, the heartbreak, paralysed to do nothing but stand.

But the death pills purred in her pocket.

Eventually, she returned to the tavern, mopping the blood of her guardian, worried she'd seen her for the last time and hadn't stopped it. One truth solidified, unable to shatter: no matter if Navira died trying, no matter if she failed, she would not rest until she saw her family again.

They wouldn't die in the Panopticon. Not if she could help it.

Content Warnings:

Graphic depictions of violence

Eye trauma

Discussions of child abuse (off page)

Gore

Discussions of Suicide

Dismemberment

Cannibalism (discussed, not seen)